Helen P. Warner

Poems of Home Life

Helen P. Warner

Poems of Home Life

ISBN/EAN: 9783337407957

Printed in Europe, USA, Canada, Australia, Japan

Cover: Foto ©Andreas Hilbeck / pixelio.de

More available books at **www.hansebooks.com**

POEMS

OF

HOME LIFE.

"Dear domestic recollections,
Home-born loves and old affections,
Incommunicable they!"

AMERICAN TRACT SOCIETY,
150 NASSAU-STREET, NEW YORK.

IT is the aim of this collection to group together some of the sweet, pure poems of our language which give expression to the varied experiences of daily life, as it flows through the channels of family and home affection, from prattling infancy to reverend age.

Through the widespread agency of the American Tract Society, may it speak tender messages to many hearts and homes.　　　　　H. P. W.

BROOKLYN.

POEMS OF HOME LIFE.

The Happy House.

"AS FOR ME AND MY HOUSE WE WILL SERVE THE LORD."

O HAPPY house ! where Thou art loved the best,
  Dear Friend and Saviour of our race ;
Where never comes such welcome honored guest,
  Where none can ever fill thy place ;
Where every heart goes forth to welcome thee,
  Where every ear attends thy word ;
Where every lip with blessings greeteth thee,
  Where all are waiting on their Lord.

O happy house ! Where man and wife in heart,
  In faith and hope are one,
That neither life nor death can ever part
  The holy union here begun ;

Where both are sharing one salvation,
　And live before thee, Lord, always,
In gladness or in tribulation,
　In happy or in evil days.

O happy house! whose little ones are given
　Early to thee, in faith and prayer—
To thee their Friend, who from the heights of heaven
　Guard'st them with more than mother's care.
O happy house! where little voices
　Their glad hosannas love to raise;
And childhood's lisping tongue rejoices
　To bring new songs of love and praise.

O happy house! and happy servitude!
　Where all alike one Master own;
Where daily duty in thy strength pursued,
　Is never hard or toilsome known;
Where each one serves thee, meek and lowly,
　Whatever thine appointment be,
Till common tasks seem great and holy,
　When they are done as unto thee.

O happy house! where thou art not forgot
　When joy is flowing full and free;
O happy house! where every wound is brought,
　Physician, Comforter, to thee;
Until at last, earth's day's work ended,
　All meet thee in that home above,
From whence thou camest, where thou hast ascended,
　Thy heaven of glory and of love!

My Home.

A THANKSGIVING TO GOD FOR A HOUSE IN THE GREEN PARISH OF
DEVONSHIRE.

LORD, thou hast given me a cell
    Wherein to dwell,
A little house, whose humble roof
    Is weather proof,
Under the sparres of which I lie,
    Both soft and drie;
Where thou, my chamber for to ward,
    Hast set a guard
Of harmlesse thoughts, to watch and keep
    Me while I sleep.
Low is my porch, as is my fate,
    Both void of state;
And yet the threshold of my doore
    Is worn by th' poore,
Who hither come and freely get
    Good words or meat.
Like as my parlor, so my hall
    And kitchen's small;
A little butterie, and therein
    A little bin,
Which keeps my little loafe of bread
    Unchipt, unstead.
Some sticks of thorn or briar
    Make me a fire,

Close by whose loving coals I sit,
    And glow like it.
Lord, I confess too, when I dine,
    The pulse is thine.
And all those other bits that bee
    There placed by thee;
The worts, the purslain, and the messe
    Of water-cresse,
Which of thy kindness thou hast sent;
    And my content
Makes those and my beloved beet
    More sweet.
Lord, 't is thy plenty-dropping hand
    That soiles my land,
And gives me, for my bushel sowne,
    Twice ten for one.
Thou mak'st my teeming hen to lay
    Her egg each day,
The while the conduits of my kine
    Run creame for wine.
All these, and better, thou dost send
    Me to this end,
That I should render for my part,
    A thankfulle heart,
Which fired with incense, I resigne
    As wholly thine;
But the acceptance, that must be,
    My CHRIST, by Thee.   R. HERRICK, 1661

Kingdom of Home.

DARK is the night, and fitful and drearily
  Rushes the wind like the waves of the sea;
Little care I, as here I sing cheerily,
  Wife at my side and my baby on knee:
    King, king, crown me the king:
    Home is the kingdom, and love is the king!

Flashes the firelight upon the dear faces,
  Dearer and dearer as onward we go,
Forces the shadows behind us, and places
  Brightness around us with warmth in the glow.
    King, king, crown me the king:
    Home is the kingdom, and love is the king!

Flashes the lovelight, increasing the glory,
  Beaming from bright eyes with warmth of the soul,
Telling of trust and content the sweet story,
  Lifting the shadows that over us roll.
    King, king, crown me the king:
    Home is the kingdom, and love is the king!

Richer than miser with perishing treasure,
  Served with a service no conquest could bring;
Happy with fortune that words cannot measure,
  Light-hearted I on the hearth-stone can sing,
    King, king, crown me the king:
    Home is the kingdom, and love is the king!

W. R. DURYEE.

What is Home?

HOME 'S not merely four square walls,
    Though hung with pictures nicely gilded;
Home is where affection calls,
    Filled with shrines the heart hath builded

Home! go watch the faithful dove,
    Sailing 'neath the heaven above us;
Home is where we 've one to love,
    Home is where there 's one to love us.

Home 's not merely roof and room;
    Home needs something to endear it;
Home is where the heart can bloom—
    Where there 's some kind heart to cheer it !

What is home with none to meet,
    None to welcome, none to greet us?
Home is sweet, and only sweet,
    When there 's *one we love* to meet us.

The Wife's Welcome.

THE hearth is swept, the fire is bright,
  The kettle sings for tea ;
The cloth is spread, the lamps alight,
The hot cakes smoke in napkins white,
  And now I wait for thee !

Come home, love, home ! thy task is done ;
  The clock ticks listeningly ;
The blinds are shut, the curtains down,
The armchair to the fireside drawn,
  Our boy upon my knee.

Thy task is done, we miss thee here ;
  Where'er thy footsteps roam,
No hand will spread such kindly cheer,
No beating heart, no listening ear
  Like those which wait at home !

Aha ! along the crisp walk fast
  That well-known step doth come ;
The bolt is drawn—the gate is passed,
The babe is wild with joy at last :
  A thousand welcomes home !   AREY.

Mercies.

MY Father ! what am I, that all
  Thy mercies sweet, like sunlight, fall
    So constant o'er my way ?

That thy great love should shelter me,
And guide my steps so tenderly
  Through every changing day?

Each morn thy light doth come and wake
My soul again, its course to take
  A day's march on with thee ;
Each night thou sendest gentle sleep,
And thine own ward and watch dost keep
  Even o'er one like me.

Thy mercy sought my wayward heart,
That long had wandered far apart
  From happiness and thee;
Thy love each day its sin forgave,
And saw but Him who died to save
  The host of those like me.

Oh, then. for His dear sake forgive
My thankless heart, and let me live
  Henceforth alone to thee !
May all my life show forth thy praise,
Assured that through its fleeting days
  Thy love shall shelter me.

No Time Like the Old Time.

THERE'S no time like the old time,
  When you and I were young,
When the buds of April blossomed,
  And the birds of springtime sung :

The garden's brightest glories
  By summer suns are nursed;
But, oh, the sweet, sweet violets,
  The flowers that opened first!

There's no place like the old place,
  Where you and I were born,
Where we lifted first our eyelids
  On the splendors of the morn,
From the milk-white breast that warmed us,
  From the clinging arms that bore,
Where the dear eyes glistened o'er us,
  That will look on us no more.

There's no friend like the old friend,
  Who has shared our morning days;
No greeting like his welcome,
  No homage like his praise!
Fame is the scentless sunflower,
  With gaudy crown of gold;
But Friendship is the breathing rose,
  With sweets in every fold.

There's no love like the old love,
  That we courted in our pride:
Though our leaves are falling, falling,
  And we're fading side by side,
There are blossoms all around us,
  With the colors of our dawn,
And we live in borrowed sunshine
  When the light of day is gone!

There are no times like the old times —
    They shall never be forgot!
There is no place like the old place;
    Keep green the dear old spot!
There are no friends like our old friends;
    May Heaven prolong their lives!
There are no loves like our old loves —
    God bless our loving wives!   o. w. HOLMES

Fifty and Fifteen.

WITH gradual gleam the day was dawning,
    Some lingering stars were seen,
When swung the garden gate behind us —
    He fifty, I fifteen!

The high-topped chaise and old gray pony
    Stood waiting in the lane;
Idly my father swayed his whip-lash,
    Lightly he held the rein.

The stars went softly back to heaven,
    The night fog rolled away,
And rims of gold and crowns of crimson
    Along the hill-top lay.

That morn the fields, they surely never
    So fair an aspect wore;
And never from the purple clover
    Such perfume rose before.

O'er hills and low romantic valleys,
　And flowing by-roads through,
I sang my simplest songs, familiar,
　That he might sing them too.

Our souls lay open to all pleasure—
　No shadow came between ;
Two children busy with their leisure,
　He fifty, I fifteen!

_____

As on my couch in languor, lonely,
　I weave beguiling rhyme,
Comes back with strangely sweet remembrance
　That far removéd time.

The slow-paced years have brought sad changes
　That morn and this between ;
And now on earth my years are fifty,
　And his in heaven fifteen.　ATLANTIC MONTHLY.

———◆———

The Old Sampler.

OUT of the way, in a corner
　Of our dear old attic room,
Where bunches of herbs from the hillside
　Shake ever a faint perfume,
An oaken chest is standing,
　With hasp and padlock and key,
Strong as the hands that made it
　On the other side of the sea.

When the winter days are dreary,
  And we 're out of heart with life,
Of its crowding cares aweary,
  And sick of its restless strife,   .
We take a lesson in patience
  From the attic corner dim.
Where the chest still holds its treasures,
  A warder faithful and grim.

Robes of an antique fashion,
  Linen and lace and silk,
That time has tinted with saffron,
  Though once they were white as milk;
Wonderful baby garments,
  'Broidered with loving care
By fingers that felt the pleasure,
  As they wrought the ruffles fair ;

A sword, with the red rust on it,
  That flashed in the battle tide,
When from Lexington to Yorktown
  Sorely men's souls were tried ;
A plumed chapeau and a buckle,
  And many a relic fine,
And all by itself the sampler,
  Framed in with berry and vine.

Faded the square of canvas,
  And dim is the silken thread,
But I think of white hands dimpled,
  And a childish, sunny head ;

For here in cross and in tent-stitch,
    In a wreath of berry and vine,
She worked it a hundred years ago,
    " Elizabeth, aged nine."

In and out in the sunshine
    The little needle flashed,
And in and out on the rainy day,
    When the merry drops down plashed,
As close she sat by her mother,
    The little Puritan maid,
And did her piece on the sampler,
    While the other children played.

You are safe in the beautiful heaven,
    " Elizabeth, aged nine ;"
But before you went you had troubles
    Sharper than any of mine.
Oh, the gold hair turned with sorrow
    White as the drifted snow,
And your tears dropped here, where I'm standing
    On this very plumed chapeau.

When you put it away, its wearer
    Would need it never more,
By a sword-thrust learning the secrets
    God keeps on yonder shore ;
And you wore your grief like glory,
    You could not yield supine,
Who wrought in your patient childhood,
    " Elizabeth, aged nine."

Out of the way, in a corner,
    With hasp and padlock and key,
Stands the oaken chest of my father's
    That came from over the sea ;
And the hillside herbs above it
    Shake odors fragrant and fine,
And here on its lid is a garland
    To "ELIZABETH, AGED NINE."

For love is of the immortal,
    And patience is sublime,
And trouble a thing of every day
    And touching every time ;
And childhood sweet and sunny,
    And womanly truth and grace,
Ever can light life's darkness
    And bless earth's lowliest place.

                MRS. M. E. SANGSTER.

Memory Bells.

SWEET memory bells! their witching chimes
  Have charms as dear as olden rhymes ;
We hear them oft at twilight hour,
When sets the sun and shuts the flower.
    O happy bells, O chiming bells,
    The clear, sweet bells of memory !

When Luna's mystic silver light
Bathes hill and dale at noon of night,

Then voices ring with magic strain,
Breaking the calm with sweet refrain.
  O happy bells, O chiming bells,
  The pure, sweet bells of memory !

Telling of childhood's joyous lays,
And hopes and fears in bygone days ;
Of bridal vows and farewells said,
And solemn dirges for the dead !
  O mournful bells, O chiming bells,
  The sad, sweet bells of memory !

Soon, soon our weary feet shall tread
That land where no sad tears are shed ;
Soon we shall clasp the hands of friends,
Where with the song no discord blends
  Of mournful bells, of tolling bells,
  The sad, sweet bells of memory ! STEWART

"When I Remember."

SORROWS humanize our race ;
  Tears are the showers that fertilize this world ;
And memory of things precious keepeth warm
The heart that once did hold them.

            They are poor
That have lost nothing ; they are poorer far
Who, losing, have forgotten ; they most poor
Of all, who lose and wish they might forget.

For life is one, and in its warp and woof
There runs a thread of gold that glitters fair,
And sometimes in the pattern shows most sweet
Where there are sombre colors.   It is true
That we have wept.   But oh ! this thread of gold,
We would not have it 'tarnish ; let us turn
Oft and look back upon the wondrous web,
And when it shineth sometimes, we shall know
That *memory is possession.*

When I remember something which I had,
   But which is gone and I must do without,
I sometimes wonder how I can be glad,
   Even in cowslip time when hedges sprout ;
It makes me sigh to think on it ; but yet
My days would not be better days should I forget.

When I remember something promised me,
   But which I never had, nor can have now,
Because the promiser I no more see
   In countries that accord with mortal vow ;
When I remember this I mourn—*but yet
My happiest days are not the days—when I forget.*

JEAN INGELOW.

The Bridge of Planks.

SPANNING the streamlet's grassy banks,
   Above the shallow brook,
  Stands the old-fashioned bridge of planks.
   In a cool, shady nook.

An alder and an aged thorn
  Over the waters meet,
And the wooden path is thin and worn
  With the tread of many feet.

For from the hamlet on the hill
  That ancient footway leads,
Over the narrow brawling rill,
  Into the wood and meads.

The sturdy laborer, hale and strong,
  Crosses with heavy tread,
While the lark trills out its morning song
  High o'er his dewy bed.

The sun-burned children, girls and boys,
  In wild and merry rout,
In the full prime of childhood's joys,
  Pass over with a shout.

The gray-haired patriarch loves the place,
  He sees it from his cot,
And totters down, with feeble pace,
  To linger near the spot.

And there, on summer eves, I ween,
  True lovers breathe their vows,
What time the pale moon's trembling sheen
  Falls on the hawthorn boughs.

Through summer's heat and winter's cold,
  Spanning the grassy banks,
It stands, the friend of young and old,
  The trusty bridge of planks.

Love Lightens Labor.

A GOOD wife rose from her bed one morn,
    And thought with a nervous dread
Of the piles of clothes to be washed, and more
    Than a dozen mouths to be fed;
Of the meals to get for the men in the field,
    And the children to fix away
To school, and the milk to be skimmed and churned;
    And all to be done that day.

It had rained in the night, and all the wood
    Was wet as it could be ;
There were puddings and pies to bake, besides
    A loaf of cake for tea.
And the day was hot, and her aching head
    Throbbed wearily as she said,
"If maidens knew what good wives know,
    They would be in no haste to wed !"

"Jennie, what do you think I told Ben Brown ?"
    Called the farmer from the well ;
And a flush crept up to his bronzéd brow,
    And his eyes half bashfully fell ;
"It was this," he said, and coming near,
    He smiled, and stooping down,
Kissed her cheek—"'t was this, that you were the best
    And the dearest wife in town !"

The farmer went back to the field, and the wife,
    In a smiling and absent way,
Sang snatches of tender little songs
    She'd not sung for many a day.

And the pain in her head was gone, and the clothes
   Were as white as the foam of the sea;
Her bread was light, and her butter was sweet,
   And golden as it could be.

"Just think," the children all called in a breath,
   "Tom Wood has run off to sea;
He would n't, I know, if he only had
   As happy a home as we."
The night came down and the good wife smiled
   To herself, as she softly said:
"'T is so sweet to labor for those we love,
   It's not strange that maids will wed!"

The Farmer's Life.

SAW ye the farmer at his plough,
   As ye were riding by,
Or wearied 'neath the noon-day toil,
   When the summer sun was high?
And thought you that his lot was hard,
   And did you thank your God
That you and yours were not condemned
   Thus like a slave to plod?

Come, see him at his harvest home,
   When garden, field and tree
Conspire with flowing store to fill
   His barn and granary.

His healthful children gayly sport
   Amid the new-mown hay,
Or proudly aid with vigorous arm
   His tasks as best they may.

The Harvest-giver is his friend,
   The Maker of the soil;
And earth, the mother, gives them bread
   And cheers their patient toil.
Come join them round their wintry hearth,
   Their heartfelt pleasure see;
And you can better judge how blest
   The farmer's life may be.   MRS. SIGOURNEY.

Country Children.

LITTLE fresh violets,
   Born in the wildwood;
Sweetly illustrating
   Innocent childhood;
Shy as the antelope—
   Brown as a berry—
Free as the mountain air,
   Romping and merry.

Blue eyes and hazel eyes
   Peep from the hedges,
Shaded by sun-bonnets
   Frayed at the edges.

Up in the apple-trees,
  Heedless of danger,
Manhood in embryo
  Stares at the stranger.

Out in the hilly patch,
  Seeking the berries—
Under the orchard tree,
  Feasting on cherries —
Tramping the clover blooms
  Down 'mong the grasses,
No voice to hinder them,
  Dear lads and lasses.

No grim propriety—
  No interdiction;
Free as the birdlings
  From city restriction !
Coining the purest blood,
  Strength'ning each muscle,
Donning health armor
  'Gainst life's coming bustle !

Dear little innocents !
  Born in the wildwood;
Oh, that all little ones
  Had such a childhood !
God's blue spread over them,
  God's green beneath them,
No sweeter heritage
  Could we bequeath them.

Living on a Farm.

HOW brightly through the mist of years,
 My quiet country home appears!
My father busy all the day
In ploughing corn or raking hay;
My mother moving with delight
Among her milk-pans, silver-bright,
We children, just from school set free,
Filling the garden with our glee.
The blood of life was flowing warm
When I was living on a farm.

I hear the sweet church-going bell,
As o'er the fields its music fell,
I see the country neighbors round
Gathering beneath the pleasant sound.
They stop awhile beside the door,
To talk their homely matters o'er—
The springing corn, the ripening grain,
And "how we need a little rain;"
"A little sun would do no harm,
We want good weather for the farm."

When autumn came, what joy to see
The gathering of the husking-bee,
To hear the voices keeping tune,
Of girls and boys beneath the moon,
To mark the golden corn-ears bright,
More golden in the yellow light!

Since I have learned the ways of men,
I often turn to these again,
And feel life wore its highest charm
When I was living on a farm.

Song of the Country Boy

WHEN my father leads his army
Of men on the harvest day,
'T is mine to carry the water,
And turn the new-mown hay.
I feel my arm grow stronger
With the toil that sweetens my food,
And I've learned to think with my mother,
That labor is noble and good.

Oh! mine is a life of pleasure,
Of sunshine and frolicsome glee,
And where is the prince on his throne
Who would not envy me?
They may talk as they will of the city,
With its streets so broad and fine,
With its palaces looking to heaven,
But I do not wish them mine.

I have heard that those mansions fair
Are the lurking dens of pride,
And those streets, by thousands trod,
Are washed by misery's tide.

And sick of the mournful story,
  With a shuddering sense of fear,
I have turned to thank my God,
  That he kindly placed me here;

That he gave to me his sunshine,
  And his winds that wander free,
And the stars, the birds and the flowers,
  Congenial friends for me ;
That he made me a free partaker
  Of the healthful, innocent joy
That tinges the sky and crowns the life
  Of the care-free country boy.

The Empty Barn.

CREAKING with laughter swings the old barn-door
  At little winking seeds upon the floor,
Dropped from four hungry barrels in a row,
Which gave their contents to make harvests grow,
While empty stalls gape with a stupid stare
At cobwebbed lofts, with loose straws dangling there:
Bunches of sunlight dance upon the floor,
About a little shoe, half-worn, beside the door;
While swaying idly from a dusty beam,
Blown by the breeze, the children's swing is seen.

An *empty barn*, save in the eaves where lies,
In little bunchy nests, guarded by watchful eyes

Great store of eggs, all speckled o'er with blue,
O'er which the birdies, quite delighted, coo,
Jealous of Sol, who curiously will peep
Between the shingles, where they lie asleep,
Wondering what warbles nestle in those shells,
Or how they 're prisoned in such little cells.

Autumn may pad its breast with fragrant store,
And peg close up the idly swinging door,
While barrels grin once more with well-fed grace.
Glad to have hoops to belt them round the waist;
And from the fields the cattle indoors stray,
With many a bleating moo and sighing neigh.
Spite of the fatness o'er the stalls' brown ribs,
And clover blossoms packed within the cribs;
Yet when 't was empty, with its laughing door
And well-filled nests, I think I loved it more.

CHARLOTTE CORDNER

Two Pictures.

AN old farmhouse, with meadows wide,
    And sweet with clover on each side;
A bright-eyed boy who looks from out
The door with woodbine wreathed about,
And wishes his one thought all day:
"Oh, if I could but fly away
    From this dull spot the world to see,
How happy, happy, happy,
    How happy I should be!"

Amid the city's constant din,
A man who round the world has been,
Who, 'mid the tumult and the throng,
Is thinking, thinking all day long:
"Oh, could I only tread once more
The field path to the farmhouse door,
   The old green meadows could I see,
How happy, nappy, happy,
   How happy I should be!"   MARIAN DOUGLAS.

Sun and Rain.

A YOUNG wife stood at the lattice-pane,
   In a study sad and "brown,"
Watching the dreary ceaseless rain
   Steadily pouring down:
     Drip, drip, drip!
   It kept on its tireless play;
And the poor little woman sighed, "Ah me!
   What a wretched, weary day!"

An eager hand at the door,
   A step as of one in haste,
A kiss on her lip once more.
   And an arm around her waist.
     Throb, throb, throb!
   Went her little heart, grateful and gay,
As she thought, with a smile, "Well, after all,
   It is n't so dull a day!"

Forgot was the plashing rain,
And the lowering skies above,
For the sombre room was lighted again
By the blessed sun of love :
"Love, love, love !"
Ran the little wife's murmured lay ;
" Without, it may threaten and frown if it will,
Within, what a golden day !"

—————

God Bless You!

HOW sweetly fall these simple words
Upon the human heart,
When friends long bound by strongest ties
Are doomed by fate to part.
Yet sadly press the hand of those
Who thus in love caress you,
And soul responsive beats to soul,
In breathing out, "God bless you !"

"God bless you !" Ah, long months ago
I heard the mournful phrase,
When one whom I in childhood loved
Went from my dreamy gaze.
Now blinding tears fall thick and fast—
I mourn my long-lost treasure,
While echoes of the heart bring back
The farewell prayer, "God bless you !"

The mother sending forth her boy
　　To scenes untried and new,
Lisps not a studied, stately speech
　　Nor murmurs out, "Adieu."
She sadly says between her sobs,
　　"Whene'er misfortunes press you,
Come to thy mother, boy, come back;"
　　Then sadly sighs, "God bless you !"

"God bless you !" more of expressed love
　　Than volumes without number,
Reveal we thus our trust in Him
　　Whose eyelids never slumber.
I ask in parting no long speech,
　　Drawled out in studied measure ;
I only ask the dear old words,
　　So sweet, so sad, "God bless you !"

Make Your Home Beautiful.

MAKE your home beautiful—bring to it flowers;
　　Plant them around you to bud and to bloom ;
Let them give light to your loneliest hours—
　　Let them bring light to enliven your gloom ;
If you can do so, oh, make it an Eden
　　Of beauty and gladness almost divine ;
'T will teach you to long for that home you are
　　　　needing,
　　The earth robed in beauty beyond this dark time.

Make home a hive, where all beautiful feelings
   Cluster like bees, and their honey-dew bring:
Make it a temple of holy revealings,
   And love its bright angel with "shadowing wings."
Then shall it be, when afar on life's billows,
   Wherever your tempest-tossed children are flung,
They will long for the shades of the home weeping-
      willow,
   And sing the sweet song which their mother had sung.

Homeless.

ALONE in the populous city!
   No hearth for my coming is warm;
And the stars, the sweet stars, are all hidden
   Away in the cloud and the storm!

The thoughts of all things that are saddest,
   The phantoms unbidden that start
From the ashes of hopes that have perished,
   Are with me to-night in my heart!

Alas, in this desolate sorrow,
   The moments are heavy and long;
And the white-pinioned spirit of fancy
   Is weary, and hushes her song.

One word of the commonest kindness
   Could make all around me seem bright
As birds in the haunts of the summer,
   Or lights in a village at night.

The Little People.

A DREARY place would be this earth,
    Were there no little people in it ;
The song of life would lose its mirth,
    Were there no children to begin it ;

No little forms, like buds to grow,
    And make the admiring heart surrender ;
No little hands on breast and brow,
    To keep the thrilling love-chords tender.

What would the mother do for work,
    Were there no pants or jackets tearing ;
No tiny dresses to embroider ;
    No cradle for their watchful caring ?

No rosy boy, at wintry morn,
    With satchel to the schoolhouse hasting :
No merry shouts, as home they rush,
    No precious morsel for their tasting ?

The sterner souls would get more stern,
    Unfeeling nature more inhuman,
And man to stoic coldness turn,
    And woman would be less than woman.

For in that clime towards which we reach
    Through time's mysterious dim unfolding,
The little ones with cherub smile
    Are still our Father's face beholding.

So said His voice in whom we trust,
　When, in Judea's realm a preacher,
He made *a child* confront the proud,
　And be in simple guise their teacher.

Life's song indeed would lose its charm,
　Were there no babies to begin it;
A doleful place this world would be,
　Were there no little people in it.'

———◆———

A Bird Song.

A LITTLE bonnie bird I know,
　With breast more soft than eider down;
A dress she wears of dappled brown,
And sings with sweeter tone, I trow—
　Ah, sweeter far this birdie sings
　Than all the birds that summer brings;
　And yet her song is only this:
　"I love you, papa!"—then a kiss.

Not tenderest song of nightingale,
　Nor sparkling trills and gurgling gush
　Of joy from velvet-throated thrush,
Nor brilliant pipe of mottled quail,
　Nor tuneful plaint of whip-poor-will,
　The measure of her song can fill;
　And yet her song is only this:
　"I love you, papa!"—then a kiss.

My Bird.

ERE last year's moon had left the sky,
    A birdling sought my Indian nest,
And folded, oh, so lovingly,
    Her tiny wings upon my breast.

From morn till evening's purple tinge,
    In winsome helplessness she lies ;
Two rose leaves, with a silken fringe,
    Shut softly on her starry eyes.

There 's not in Ind a lovelier bird—
    Broad earth owns not a happier nest.
O God, thou hast a fountain stirred,
    Whose waters nevermore shall rest !

This beautiful, mysterious thing,
    This seeming visitant from heaven,
This bird with the immortal wing,
    To me—to *me* thy hand has given.

The pulse first caught its tiny stroke,
    The blood its crimson hue from mine ;
This life which I have dared invoke,
    Henceforth is parallel with thine.

A silent awe is in my room,
    I tremble with delicious fear ;
The future—with its light and gloom,
    Time and Eternity—is here.

Doubts—hopes, in eager tumult rise :
Hear, O my God, one earnest prayer!
Room for my bird in Paradise ;
And give her angel plumage there !

BUUMAH, 1848.   EMILY C. JUDSON.

Choosing a Name.

I HAVE got a new-born sister;
I was nigh the first that kissed her
When the nursing-woman brought her
To papa—his infant daughter !
And papa has made the offer,
I shall have the naming of her.

Now I wonder what would please her—
Charlotte, Julia, or Louisa ?
Ann and Mary, they 're too common;
Joan 's too formal for a woman;
Jane 's a prettier name beside;
But we had a Jane that died.
They would say, if 't was Rebecca,
That she was a little Quaker.
Edith 's pretty, but that looks
Better in old English books;
Ellen 's left off long ago;
Blanche is out of fashion now.
None that I have named as yet
Are so good as Margaret.

Emily is neat and fine;
What do you think of Caroline?
How I'm puzzled and perplexed
What to choose or think of next!
I am in a little fever
Lest the name that I should give her
Should disgrace her or defame her;
I will leave papa to name her.　　　MARY LAMB.

Weighing the Baby.

HOW many pounds does the baby weigh,
　　Baby who came but a month ago?
How many pounds from the crowning curl
　　To the rosy point of the restless toe?"

Grandfather ties the 'kerchief's knot,
　　Tenderly guides the swinging weight,
And carefully over his glasses peers
　　To read the record, "Only eight."

Softly the echo goes around;
　　The father laughs at the tiny girl,
The fair young mother sings the words,
　　While grandmother smoothes the golden curl.

And stooping above the precious thing,
　　Nestles a kiss within a prayer,
Murmuring softly, "Little one,
　　Grandfather did not weigh you fair."

Nobody weighed the baby's smile,
　Or the love that came with the helpless one;
Nobody weighed the threads of care
　From which a woman's life is spun.

No index tells the mighty worth
　Of little baby's quiet breath,
A soft, unceasing metronome,
　Patient and faithful unto death.

Nobody weighed the baby's soul,
　For here on earth no weight may be
That could avail; God only knows
　Its value in eternity.

Only eight pounds to hold a soul
　That seeks no angel's silver wing,
But shines beneath this human guise,
　Within so small and frail a thing !

O mother, laugh your merry note ;
　Be gay and glad, but don't forget
From baby eyes looks out a soul
　That claims a home in Eden yet.

MRS. E. L. BEERS.

Mother's Song.

DON'T grow old too fast, my sweet!
　　Stay a little while
　In this pleasant baby-land,
　　Sunned by mother's smile.

Grasp not with thy dimpled hands
  At the world outside;
They are still too rosy soft,
  Life too cold and wide.

Be not wistful, sweet blue-eyes!
  Find your rest in mine,
Which through life shall watchful be
  To keep all tears from thine.

Be not restless, little feet!
  Lie within my hand;
Far too round these tiny soles
  Yet to try to stand.

For awhile be mine alone,
  So helpless and so dear;
By-and-by thou must go forth,
  But now, sweet, slumber here

———◆———

Hae Shoon.

NAE shoon to hide her tiny tae,
  Nae stocking on her feet,
Her supple ankles white as snaw,
  Like early blossoms sweet.

Her simple dress of sprinkled pink,
  Her double, dimpled chin,
Her puckered lips and balmy mou',
  With nae one tooth between.

Her e'en sae like her mither's e'en,
　Twa gentle liquid things;
Her face is like an angel's face—
　We're glad she has nae wings!

She is the budding of our love,
　A giftie God has gied us;
We munna love the gift o'er weel,
　'Twad be nae blessing to us.

———◆———

Where's My Baby?

WHERE'S my baby?　Where's my baby?
　But a little while ago,
In my arms I held one fondly,
　And a robe of lengthened flow
Covered little knees so dimpled,
　And each pink and chubby toe.

Where's my baby?　I remember
　Now about the shoes so red,
Peeping from his shortened dresses,
　And the bright curls on his head ;
Of the little teeth so pearly,
　And the first sweet words he said.

Where's my baby?　In the door yard
　Is a boy with shingled hair,
Whittling, as he tries to whistle,
　With a big boy's manly air,

With his pants within his boot-tops.
  But my baby is not there.

Where's my baby?—Ask that urchin,
  Let me hear what he will say:
"Where's your baby, ma?" he questioned,
  With a roguish look and way;
"Guess he's grown to be a boy, now,
  Big enough to work and play."

Where's my baby? Where's my baby?
  Ah! the years fly on apace !
Yesterday I held and kissed it,
  In its loveliness and grace;
But to-morrow sturdy manhood
  Takes the little baby's place.

Baby's Shoes.

OH those little, those little blue shoes!
  Those shoes that no little feet use.
      Oh the price were high
      That those shoes would buy,
  Those little blue unused shoes !

For they hold the small shape of feet
That no more their mother's eye meet,
      That, by God's good will,
      Years since grew still,
And ceased from their totter so sweet.

And oh, since that baby slept,
So hushed, how the mother has kept,
　　With a tearful pleasure,
　　That dear little treasure,
And o'er them thought and wept !

For they mind her evermore
Of a patter along the floor,
　　And blue eyes she sees
　　Look up from her knees
With the look that in life they wore.

As they lie before her there,
There babbles from chair to chair
　　A little sweet face
　　That's a gleam in the place,
With its little gold curls of hair.

Then oh wonder not that her heart
From all else would rather part
　　Than those tiny blue shoes
　　That no little feet use,
And whose sight makes such fond tears start.

W. C. BENNETT

That Baby over the Way.

AS I 've sat at my chamber window,
　　I 've noticed, again and again,
The sweetest of baby figures,
　　At the opposite window-pane ;

Rosy cheeks daintily dimpled,
   Curls that, without any check,
Tumble and twist in confusion,
   With the corals about its neck.

Eyes—but to mention the color,
   I must wait for a nearer view,
Though I think I may state, at a venture,
   They'll match with the ribbons of blue
Feet with their tiny bronzed slippers,
   And the dearest of wee chubby fists,
And arms, in whose foldings of fatness
   You must search for the little one's wrist

Sometimes I throw kisses to baby,
   And back come the kisses to me ;
And the intricate game of "bo-peep"
   Is a source of infinite glee,
That lights up the smiles and the dimples ;
   So I think I may truthfully say,
That I have an established flirtation
   With the baby over the way.

But how has the little one stolen
   A march on my foolish old heart?
And why, as I watch those bright eyes,
   Will the quick tear instinctively start?
Ah, because in the long ago years,
   Ere time mixed my tresses with gray,
I, too, had a baby as lovely
   As the little one over the way.

From the white robe and clustering curls,
 From that vision of infantine joy,
Oh, sadly, so sadly I turn
 To all I have left of *my* boy·
To the baby-clothes, yellow with age,
 To the curl that once lay on his brow,
To the old-fashioned cradle—the nest
 So drearily tenantless now.

The first grief comes back to me then,
 The longing that cannot be told,
For the sight of the dear little face,
 For my own darling baby to hold ;
And my arms ache with emptiness so
 That I feel I am hardly content
To wait for the summons to go
 The way that my little one went.

And so, for the sake of the joy
 That long ago gladdened my heart,
For the light that once shone on my way
 So quickly, alas ! to depart ;
For the love that I bore my one darling,
 All babies are dearer to-day ;
And I think I must call on the mother
 Of that baby over the way.

Three Little Chairs.

THEY sat alone by the bright wood fire,
The gray-haired dame and the aged sire,
   Dreaming of days gone by ;
The tear-drops fell on each wrinkled cheek,
They both had thoughts they could not speak,
   As each heart uttered a sigh.

For their sad and tearful eyes descried
Three little chairs, placed side by side,
   Against the sitting-room wall ;
Old-fashioned enough as there they stood,
Their seats of flag and their frames of wood,
   With their backs so straight and tall.

Then the father shook his silvery head,
And with trembling voice he gently said .
   "Mother, those empty chairs !
They bring us such sad, sad thoughts to-night,
We 'll put them for ever out of sight,
   In the small dark room up-stairs."

But she answered, "Father, no, not yet,
For I look at them, and I forget
   That the children went away ;
The boys come back, and our Mary, too,
With her apron on of checkered blue,
   And sit here every day.

"Johnny still whittles a ship's tall masts,
And Willie his leaden bullets casts,
  While Mary her patchwork sews :
At evening time three childish prayers
Go up to God from those little chairs,
  So softly that no one knows.

"Johnny comes back from the billowy deep,
Willie wakes from his battle-field sleep,
  To say a good-night to me :
Mary 's a wife and a mother no more,
But a tired child whose playtime is o'er,
  And comes to rest on my knee.

"So let them stand there, though empty now,
And every time when alone we bow
  At the Father's throne to pray,
We 'll ask to meet the children above,
In our Saviour's home of rest and love,
  Where no child goeth away."

The Children.

WHEN the lessons and tasks are all ended,
  And the school for the day is dismissed,
And the little ones gather around me,
  To bid me good-night and be kissed.
Oh, the little white arms that encircle
  My neck in a tender embrace !
Oh, the smiles that are halos of heaven,
  Shedding sunshine of love on my face !

And when they are gone I sit dreaming
    Of my childhood too lovely to last;
Of love that my heart will remember
    When it wakes to the pulse of the past,
Ere the world and its wickedness made me
    A partner of sorrow and sin;
When the glory of God was about me,
    And the glory of gladness within.

Oh, my heart grows weak as a woman's,
    And the fountains of feeling will flow,
When I think of the paths steep and stony,
    Where the feet of the dear ones must go;
Of the mountains of sin hanging o'er them,
    Of the tempest of fate blowing wild;
Oh, there's nothing of earth half so holy
    As the innocent heart of a child.

They are idols of hearts and of households.
    They are angels of God in disguise;
His sunlight still sleeps in their tresses,
    His glory still gleams in their eyes:
Oh, those truants from home and from heaven
    They have made me more manly and mild.
And I know how Jesus could liken
    The kingdom of God to a child.

I ask not a life for the dear ones,
    All radiant, as others have done,
But that life may have just enough shadow
    To temper the glare of the sun.

I would pray God to guard them from evil,
  But my prayer would bound back to myself;
Ah, a seraph may pray for a sinner,
  But a sinner must pray for himself.

The twig is so easily bended,
  I have banished the rule and the rod;
I have taught them the goodness of knowledge,
  They have taught me the goodness of God.
My heart is a dungeon of darkness,
  Where I shut them from breaking a rule;
My frown is sufficient correction;
  My love is the law of the school.

I shall leave the old house in the autumn,
  To traverse its threshold no more:
Ah, how shall I sigh for the dear ones
  That meet me each morn at the door.
I shall miss the "good nights" and the kisses,
  And the gush of their innocent glee,
The group on the green, and the flowers
  That are brought every morning to me.

I shall miss them at morn and at eve,
  Their song in the school and the street;
I shall miss the low hum of their voices,
  And the tramp of their delicate feet.
When the lessons and tasks are all ended,
  And Death says, "The school is dismissed!"
May the little ones gather around me,
  To bid me good night and be kissed!

Rebuke.

THE world is old and the world is cold,
 And never a day is fair, I said.
Out of the heavens the sunlight rolled,
 The green leaves rustled above my head,
And the sea was a sea of gold.

"The world is cruel," I said again ;
 "Her voice is harsh to my shrinking ear,
And the nights are dreary and full of pain."
 Out of the darkness, sweet and clear,
There rippled a tender strain—

Rippled the song of a bird asleep,
 That sang in a dream of the budding wood,
Of shining fields where the reapers reap,
 Of a wee brown mate and a nestling brood,
And the grass where the berries peep.

"The world is false though the world be fair,
 And never a heart is pure," I said.
And lo ! the clinging of white arms bare,
 The innocent gold of my baby's head,
And the lisp of a childish prayer.

Bedtime.

A ROW of little faces by the bed,
 A row of little hands upon the spread ;
A row of little roguish eyes all closed,
A row of little naked feet exposed.

A gentle mother leads them in their praise,
Teaching their feet to tread in heavenly ways,
And takes this lull in childhood's tiny tide,
The little errors of the day to chide.

No lovelier sight this side of heaven is seen,
And angels hover o'er the group serene ;
Instead of odors in a censer swung,
There floats the fragrance of an infant's tongue.

Then tumbling headlong into waiting beds,
Beneath the sheets they hide their timid heads,
Till slumber hides away their idle fears,
And like a peeping bud each face appears.

All dressed like angels in their gowns of white,
They 're wafted to the skies in dreams of light,
And heaven will sparkle in their eyes at morn,
And stolen graces all their ways adorn.

A Song to bring Sleep.

TWO little eyes,
  Two little lips,
    Two little hands,
    Two little feet:
What shall we ask for them all ?

    Two little eyes,
      Blue, blue,
Blue as the azure deep of the skies—
Now so roguish, now wondrous wise,

Solemn and funny, all in a twink,
Changing and changing with every wink :
What shall we ask for these little eyes?

Open them, Lord,
To see in thy word,
Wondrous things ;
Light them with love,
And shade them above
With angel's wings.

Two little lips,
Red, red,
Red as the flamy coral tips,
Sweet as the rose the wild bee sips,
Singing and prattling all day long,
And kissing and coaxing with witchery strong :
What shall we ask for these little lips?

From thine altar, Lord, above,
Touch those lips with fire of love ;
Pure, pure let them be,
Speaking holy melodies
Out of a holy heart that rise,
Warm, bright, up to thee !

Two little hands,
Busy, busy,
Busy as bird, and busy as bee,
Gathering "funny things" for me.

Weaving webs, and building a house
"Just the size for a wee, wee mouse :"
What shall we ask for these little hands?

Lord, with wisdom filled,
Teach these hands to build
    Thine own temple ;
Let them skilful be—
Cunning to work for thee
    By thine example.

Two little feet,
Nimble, nimble,
Trot-foot and Light-foot, oh, what a pair ;
Now here, now there, now everywhere :
Running of errands, dancing in glee,
Skipping and jumping merrily :
What shall we ask for these little feet?

Lead them a blessed pilgrimage,
From childhood through to saintly age,
    Dear Lord, we pray :
Hold them a light in the dim, dark night,
And out of the narrow path of the right
Ne'er let them stray !

Two little eyes—closed !
Two little lips—shut !
Two little hands—clasped !
Two little feet—still !
God give my darling pleasant dreams !

REV. J. K. NUTTING.

Little Children.

CANDID and curious, how they seek
  All truth to know and scan;
    And ere the budding mind can speak,
      Begin to study man !
Confiding sweetness colors all they say,
And angels listen when they try to pray.

    More playful than the birds of spring,
      Ingenuous, warm, sincere;
    Like meadow-bees upon the wing
      They roam without a fear;
And breathe their thoughts on all who round them
    live,
As light sheds beams, or flowers their perfume give.

MONTGOMERY

"Open your Mouth and Shut your Eyes."

OPEN your mouth and shut your eyes,"
    Three little maidens were saying,
  "And see what God sends you !" Little they thought
    He listened while they were playing ;
So little we guess that a light, light word
    At times may be more than praying.

' I," said Kate, with merry blue eyes,
  "Would have lots of frolic and folly."
" I," said Lu, with the bonnie brown hair,
  "Would have life always smiling and jolly."
" And I would have just what our Father may send,"
  Said lovable little pale Polly.

Life came for the two, with sweetnesses new,
  Every morning in gloss and in glister,
But our Father above, in a gush of great love,
  Caught up little Polly and kissed her.
And the churchyard nestled another wee grave;
  The angels another wee sister.   GERALD MASSEY.

The Little Grave.

YOU need not dig it very wide,
  Nor dig it very deep,
The little grave in which to hide
  My baby—gone to sleep.

But dig it where the sun will shine
  Upon it all the day,
And birds and blossoms all combine
  To drive the gloom away.

Choose some fair spot, where, in spring
  The grass will soonest grow;
And where the robins first will sing,
  And daisy blossoms blow.

And take some violets from the brook,
  And plant them at her head;
Her eyes had just their dewy look—
  Our violet is dead.

How slow the days will come and go,
  Now baby's gone away;
But God will love her best, I know,
  Although I weep to-day.

Little Boy's Pocket.

DO you know what's in my pottet?
  Such a lot of treasures in it !
  Listen now while I bedin it;
  Such a lot of sings it hold,
And every sing dat's in my pottet,
And when, and where, and how I dot it.

First of all, here's in my pottet
  A beauty shell—I picked it up;
  And here's the handle of a tup
  That somebody has broke at tea;
  The shell's a hole in it, you see;
Nobody knows dat I dot it,
I keep it safe here in my pottet.

And here's my ball, too, in my pottet,
  And here's my pennies, one, two, free,
  'That Aunty Mary gave to me;

To-morrow day I'll buy a spade,
When I'm out walking with the maid;
I can't put dat here in my pottet,
But I can use it when I've dot it.

Here's some more sings in my pottet!
Here's my lead, and here's my string,
And once I had an iron ring,
But through a hole it lost one day;
And this is what I always say—
A hole's the worst sing in a pottet;
Have it mended when you've dot it.

The Grain of Corn and the Penny.

A GRAIN of corn an infant's hand
May plant upon an inch of land,
Whence twenty stalks may spring, and yield
Enough to stock a little field.
The harvest of that field might then
Be multiplied to ten times ten,
Which, sown thrice more, would furnish bread,
Wherewith an army might be fed.

A penny is a little thing,
Which e'en the poor man's child may fling
Into the treasury of heaven,
And make it worth as much as seven.
As seven? nay, worth its weight in gold,
And that increased a million-fold ·

For lo, a penny tract, if well
Applied, may save a soul from hell.
That soul can scarce be saved alone;
It must, it will, its bliss make known.
"Come," it will cry, "and you shall see
What great things God has done for me!"
Hundreds that joyful sound may hear—
Hear with the heart as well as ear;
And these to thousands more proclaim
Salvation in the "Only Name;"
Till every tongue and tribe shall call
On "Jesus" as the Lord of all.

JAMES MONTGOMERY.

"Was 'oo Ever a Boy?"

MY little four-year-old Harry,
     Bright in beauty and joy,
Said with his accent of wonder,
     "Papa, was 'oo ever a boy?
Was 'oo ever as little as I be?"
     "Dear baby," I said, in reply,
"Will my darling ever be weary
     And heart-worn, and sinful as I?"

With forehead of whiteness and candor,
     And loving and innocent eyes,
Thou dost measure the distance between us
     With a strange and holy surprise.

Thou like a bud flushed and fragrant,
  I like a leaf at its fall ;
I far away from the angels,
  Thou within reach of their call.

Type of the beauty celestial,
  Humble, and tender, and sweet,
Thou comest in faith, my darling,
  To sit at thy father's feet.
Taught by thy loving example,
  By thy truth that knows no alloy,
May I go to our Father as simply,
  And in heart be always a boy.

FANNY DARTON.

----·----

Little Goldenhair.

GOLDENHAIR climbed up on grandpapa's knee,
  Dear little Goldenhair ! tired was she,
All the day busy as busy could be.

Up in the morning as soon as 't was light ;
Out with the birds and the butterflies bright,
Skipping about till the coming of night.

Grandpapa toyed with the curls on her head.
" What has my baby been doing," he said,
" Since she arose with the sun from her bed ?"

"Pitty much," answered the sweet little one.
"I cannot tell, so much things I have done;
Played with my dolly, and feeded my Bun.

"And I have readed in my picture-book,
And little Bella and I went to look
For some smooth stones by the side of the brook.

"Then I comed home, and I eated my tea,
And I climbed up to my grandpapa's knee—
I jes' as tired as tired can be!"

Lower and lower the little head pressed,
Until it drooped upon grandpapa's breast.
Dear little Goldenhair, sweet be thy rest!

———

We are as children; the things that we do
Are as sports of a babe to the Infinite view
That marks all our weakness, and pities it too.

God grant that when night overshadows our way,
And we shall be called to account for our day,
He may find it as guileless as Goldenhair's play.

And oh! when aweary, may we be so blest
As to sink, like an innocent child, to our rest,
And feel ourselves clasped to the Infinite Breast.

F. BURGE SMITH.

Daisy's Prayer.

DARLING little Daisy,
   With her golden hair
Sitting at the table
   In her own high chair,

Closed the dewy eyelids
   Over blue eyes bright;
Drooped the golden lashes
   Over cheeks so white,

Bent above the table
   Little head so fair ;
Daisy's supper's waiting
   Till she says her prayer.

So she clasps her fingers
   As when wont to pray ;
"Oh, dear me," sighs Daisy,
   "What does papa say ?"

Lower bows her forehead
   O'er the table then ;
And she whispers softly,
   "Jesus' sake, Amen."

Darling little Daisy,
   With your winsome face,
May the blessed Saviour
   Daily give his grace !

May you never venture
    Any path-to take,
Till you ask God's blessing
    For dear Jesus' sake.

When the light of childhood
    Shall have left your brow,
May your faith in Jesus
    Be as pure as now !

From all sin and wandering
    May good angels keep !
And at last in Jesus
    May you fall asleep.

Only a Boy.

ONLY a boy, with his noise and fun,
    The veriest mystery under the sun ;
    As brimful of mischief, and wit, and glee,
    As ever a human frame can be,
    And as hard to manage as—what? ah me !
        'Tis hard to tell,
        Yet we love him well.

Only a boy, with his fearful tread,
    Who cannot be driven, but must be led ;
    Who troubles the neighbors' dogs and cats,
    And tears more clothes, and spoils more hats
    Loses more tops, and kites, and bats,
        Than would stock a store
        For a year or more.

Only a boy, with his wild, strange ways,
With his idle hours and his busy days ;
With his queer remarks, and his odd replies,
Sometimes foolish, and sometimes wise,
Often brilliant, for one of his size,
    As a meteor hurled
    From the planet world.

Only a boy, who will be a man,
If nature goes on with its first great plan—
If water, or fire, or some fatal snare,
Conspire not to rob us of this our heir,
Our blessing, our trouble, our rest, our care,
    Our torment, our joy !
    "Only a boy."

Woman's Work.

DARNING little stockings
    For restless little feet ;
Washing little faces
    To keep them clean and sweet ;
Hearing Bible lessons ;
    Teaching catechism ;
Praying for salvation
    From heresy and schism—
        Woman's work.

Sewing on the buttons;
  Overseeing rations;
Soothing with a kind word
  Others lamentations;
Guiding clumsy Bridgets,
  And coaxing sullen cooks;
Entertaining company,
  And reading recent books—
        Woman's work.

Burying out of sight
  Her own unhealing smarts,
Letting in the sunshine
  On other clouded hearts;
Binding up the wounded,
  And healing of the sick;
Bravely marching onward
  Through dangers dark and thick—
        Woman's work.

Leading little children,
  And blessing manhood's years.
Showing to the sinful
  How God's forgiveness cheers;
Scattering sweet roses
  Along another's path;
Smiling by the wayside,
  Content with what she hath—
        Woman's work.

Letting fall her own tears
    Where only God can see ;
Wiping off another's
    With tender sympathy ;
Learning by experience ;
    Teaching by example ;
Yearning for the gateway,
    Golden, pearly, ample—
        Woman's work.

Fresh grave in the valley—
    Tears, bitter sobs, regret ;
One more solemn lesson
    That life may not forget.
Face for ever hidden,
    Race for ever run—
" Dust to dust," a voice saith,
    And woman's work is done.

Mrs. Lofty and I.

MRS. LOFTY keeps a carriage,
      So do I ;
She has dapple grays to draw it,
      None have I ;
With my blue-eyed laughing baby,
      Trundling by,
I hide his face, lest she should see
The cherub boy, and envy me.

Her fine husband has white fingers,
     Mine has not;
He could give his bride a palace—
     Mine a cot;
Hers comes home beneath the starlight -
     Ne'er cares she;
Mine comes in the purple twilight,
     Kisses me;
And prays that He who turns life's sands
Will hold his loved ones in his hands.

Mrs. Lofty has her jewels,
     So have I;
She wears hers upon her bosom—
     Inside I;
She will leave hers at death's portal
     By-and-by;
I shall bear my treasure with me
     When I die;
For I have love and she has gold:
She counts her wealth—mine can't be told.

She has those who love her station,
     None have I;
But I've one true heart beside me:
     Glad am I;
I'd not change it for a kingdom,
     No, not I;
God will weigh it in his balance,
     By-and-by;
And the difference define
'Twixt Mrs. Lofty's wealth and mine.

Cradle Song.

,'T IS night on the mountain,
　　'T is night on the sea,
Mild dewdrops are kissing
　　The bloom-covered lea ;
Like plumes gently waving,
　　The soft zephyrs creep ;
The birds are all dreaming—
　　Then sleep, darling, sleep.

'T is night on the mountain.
　　'T is night on the sea,
Away in the distance
　　The stars twinkle free ;
O'er all of His creatures
　　His watch He will keep
Who guardeth the sparrows—
　　Then sleep, darling, sleep.

MARY M BOWEN.

Love versus Wealth.

M ARRY not for wealth,
　　Whate'er be thy lot ;
For gold is but pelf
　　Where love is not.

Stoop thou not to take
　　A princess' hand,
If not *for thy sake*
　　She 'll by thee stand.

Marry thou for love,
By truth be led;
Toil and look above
For daily bread.

ILOYD.

Giving in Marriage.

TO bear, to nurse, to rear,
   To watch, and then to lose;
To see my bright ones disappear,
   Drawn up like morning dews:
To bear, to nurse, to rear,
   To watch, and then to lose:
This have I done when God drew near
   Among his own to choose.

To hear, to heed, to wed,
   And with thy lord depart,
In tears that he, as soon as shed,
   Will let no longer smart:
To hear, to heed, to wed,
   This while thou didst I smiled;
For now it was not God who said,
   "Mother, give ME thy child!"

O fond, O fool, and blind!
   To God I gave with tears;
But when a man like grace would find,
   My soul put by her fears:

O fond, O fool, and blind !
  God guards in happier spheres ;
That man will guard where he did bind,
  Is hope for unknown years.

To hear, to heed, to wed,
  Fair lot that maidens choose !
Thy mother's tenderest words are said,
  · Thy face no more she views :
Thy mother's lot, my dear,
  She doth in naught accuse ;
Her lot to bear, to nurse, to rear,
  To love—and then to lose ! JEAN INGELOW.

A Bridal Benediction.

SO fair the scene when hearts agree,
  When vows are breathed and pledges given :
So sweet are weddings—can it be
  That there are none in heaven ?

Not wedded love—a purer gleam,
  To bless the world of light, is given ;
Earth's love is but a troubled stream
  To the clear depth of heaven.

Yet wedlock is a boon divine,
  To Eden's rosy bowers first given ;
And love's dear Lord, at Cana's shrine,
  Renewed the seal of heaven.

Come then, O heavenly Guest, this day;
　Thy blessing at these nuptials given,
The angels bending down shall say,
　This might have been in heaven.

These two young lives together wrought,
　New years begun, a new home given,
Transfused in mind, in heart, and thought,
　'T is a sweet type of heaven.

Both lambs of the good Shepherd's care,
　Both to the ark of safety driven;
Such wedded love the blest might share,
　Such chains be worn in heaven.

Dear Lord, oh keep them near to thee;
　To them a deep, sweet peace be given;
So living here that each shall be
　The spouse of Christ in heaven.

F. M. CAULKINS.

Where is Jamie?

FATHER, where is our Jamie to-night—
　Jamie, so bold and so gay?
The twilight shadows are falling now,
　Why does he stay away?
Jamie is handsome, and manly too,
　And he will be good and great.
But, father, why is our darling boy
　A staying away so late?"

"Our noble boy is a child no more,
    He has grown to man's estate ;
He has gone a courting Minnie Gray,
    The reason he stays so late.
For her golden hair and eyes of blue
    Have stolen his heart away ;
And he goes in the holy twilight hour
    A wooing sweet Minnie Gray."

"Why does the maiden lure him away,
    Now we are growing so old?
And we have shielded him all his life—
    Our love has never grown cold.
The maiden can never love as we
    Have loved him all his years,
Who have led him along the path of life.
    Sharing his smiles and tears."

"But, Millie, remember long years ago,
    When I was handsome and gay,
And you a maiden so fair and sweet
    That you stole my heart away.
I had a father old and gray,
    And a mother kind and true,
Who loved me fondly all my life—
    But my heart went out with you."

A blush crept over her withered cheek,
    Her eye shone clear and mild ;
No longer she chided the lovely maid
    For winning away her child.

She thought of the long ago, when she
    Stood close to her lover's side,
In the little church, and the man of God
    Made her a happy bride.

Yesterday.

WHAT makes the king unhappy?
    His queen is young and fair,
His children climb around him,
    With waving yellow hair.

His realm is broad and peaceful,
    He fears no foreign foe ;
And health to his veins comes leaping
    In all the winds that blow.

What makes the king unhappy?
    Alas ! a little thing
That money cannot purchase,
    Or fleets and armies bring.

And yesterday he had it.
    With yesterday it went ;
And yesterday it perished,
    With all the king's content.

For this he sits lamenting,
    And sighs, "Alack ! alack !
I 'd give one half my kingdom
    Could yesterday come back !"

To-Day.

EVERY new day has its dawn,
 Its soft and silent eve,
Its noontide hour of bliss or bale—
 Wherefore should we grieve?

Why do we heap huge mounds of years
 Before us and behind,
And scorn the little days that pass
 Like angels on the wind?

Each turning round a small sweet face
 As beautiful as near;
Because it is so small a face
 We will not see it clear;

We will not clasp it as it flies,
 And kiss its lips and brow;
We will not bathe our wearied souls
 In its delicious now.

And so it turns from us, and goes
 Away in sad disdain,
Though we would give our lives for it,
 It never comes again.

Yet every new day has its dawn,
 Its noontide, and its eve:
Live while we live, giving God thanks—
 He will not let us grieve. MRS. D. M. CRAIK

To-morrow.

A BRIGHT little boy with laughing face,
Whose every motion was full of grace,
Who knew no trouble and feared no care,
Was the light of our household — the youngest
    there.

He was too young, this little elf,
With troublesome questions to vex himself;
But for many days a thought would arise,
And bring a shade to the dancing eyes.

He went to one whom he thought more wise
Than any other beneath the skies ;
"Mother," O word that makes the home !
"Tell me, when will to-morrow come ?"

"It is almost night." the mother said,
"And time for my boy to be in bed ;
When you wake up and it 's day again,
It will be to-morrow, my darling, then."

The little boy slept through all the night,
But woke with the first red streak of light ;
He pressed a kiss to his mother's brow,
And whispered "Is it to-morrow now ?"

"No, little Eddie. this is to-day ,
To-morrow is always one night away :"
He pondered awhile, but joys came fast,
And this vexing question quickly passed.

But it came again with the shades of night;
"Will it be to-morrow when it is light?"
From years to come he seemed care to borrow,
He tried so hard to catch to-morrow.

"You cannot catch it, my little Ted;
Enjoy to-day," the mother said;
"Some wait for to-morrow through many a year -
It always is coming, but never is here."

MRS. M. R. JOHNSON.

To-morrow.

'TIS late at night—and in the realms of sleep
My little lambs are folded like the flocks;
From room to room I hear the wakeful clocks
Challenge the passing hour, like guards that keep
Their solitary watch on tower and steep;
Far off I hear the crowing of the cocks,
And through the opening door that time unlocks,
Feel the fresh breathing of to-morrow creep.

To-morrow! the mysterious unknown guest,
Who cries aloud; "Remember Barmicide,
And tremble to be happy with the rest!"
And I make answer: "I am satisfied;
I dare not ask—I know not what is best;
God hath already said what shall betide."

LONGFELLOW.

Birthdays.

BRIGHT birthdays in the happy home!
  And tender love prepares
Fond gifts to please the precious child
  That dwelleth on its prayers.
It showereth o'er the blooming youth
  Blessings and tokens sweet,
And bows before the hoary head
  To pay an offering meet.

The birthday of the absent! Thought
  On wingéd scroll shall fly
To distant realms, or stranger climes
  Beneath a foreign sky;
Or bear that love o'er ocean waves
  That fierce with anger frown,
Which many waters cannot quench,
  Nor all their billows drown.

The birthday of the dead! Be sure
  That sacred date to keep;
Send portions to the sick and poor,
  And dry the eyes that weep;
Wrap garments round the shrinking form,
  Homes for the orphan find,
And bid the light of knowledge beam
  Upon the darkened mind.

Spread wide the page that speaks of God;
  Speed on the mission band

O'er western vales, o'er Asia's wilds,
　Or far Liberia's strand :
Give teachers to the prairie child,
　Shed hope o'er souls forlorn,
Speak kindly words to erring hearts
　That feel the sting of scorn.

Remember those who climb the shroud
　And plough the surging main ;
Breathe pity through the prison grate
　On sin's despairing train :
For all mankind let deeds and prayers
　Of pure good-will be given ;
So shall the birthdays of the dead
　Help thine own soul to heaven.

MRS. SIGOURNEY.

The Twentieth Birthday.

GIRLHOOD'S sunny days are over
　　With to-day ;
They with all their wayward brightness,
　　Pass away :
Woman's earnest path before me
　　Lieth straight.
Who can tell what grief and anguish
　　There await ?

Guide me, Father, God of mercy,
　　On the way ;
Never from thy holy guidance
　　Let me stray :

Give that meed of joy or sorrow
    Pleaseth thee,
Whatsoe'er thy will ordaineth
    Best for me.

In the shadow and the darkness
    Be my star ;
In the light, lest radiance dazzle,
    Go not far ;
Make me patient, kind, and gentle,
    Day by day ;
Teach me how to live more nearly
    As I pray.

What my heart so much desireth,
    Grant me still,
If that earnest hope accordeth
    With thy will :
Should thy mercy quite withhold it,
    Be thou near :
Let me feel I hold its promise
    All too dear.

Here, upon life's very threshold,
    Take my heart ;
From thy holy guidance let it
    Ne'er depart ;
When life's stormy strife is over,
    Take me home,
There to be more fully, truly,
    Thine alone.

Life and I.

LIFE is the child's frail wreath,
  And I a drop of dew
Upon its fading beauty. In the breath
  Of the still night-air come I forth to view;
But with the reddening morn,
I silently return
To holy realms unseen,
Where death hath never been,
Where He hath his abode,
Who is my God!

Life is the wind-snapped bough,
  And I a little bird—
My motherland a fairer, calmer clime,
  Whose olive groves no storm has ever stirred:
A little bird that came from far,
Beyond the evening star,
Alighting in my untried flight
Upon this tree of night.
Yet ere another sun
His race shall have begun,
I shall have passed from sight,
To realms of truer light,
These twilight skies above,
To be with Him I love,
My Lord, my God.

Life is the mountain lake,
  And I a drifting cloud,
Or a cloud's broken shadow on the wave,
  One of the silent multitude that crowd,
With ever-varying pace,
Across the water's face!
Soon must I pass from earth,
To the calm azure of my better birth,
My sky of holy bliss;
With Him in love and peace   .
To have my long abode,
Who is my God.

Life is the tossing ark,
  And I the wandering dove,
Resting to-day mid clouds and waters dark,
  To-morrow in my peaceful olive grove
Returning in glad haste
Across time's billowy waste,
For evermore to rest
Upon the faithful breast
Of Him who is my king,
My Christ, my God.

Life is the changing deep,
  And I a little wave,
Rising a moment, and then passing down
  Amid my fellows to a peaceful grave:
For this is not my rest,
It is not here I can be blest.

Far from this sea of strife,
With Christ is hid my life,
With Christ my glorious Lord,
My King and God!

Life is a well-strung lyre,
  And I a wandering note,
Struck from its cunning chords, and left alone
  A moment in the quivering air to float;
Then, without echo, die,
And upward from this earthly jarring fly,
To form a truer note above,
In the great song of joy and love,
The never-ending, never-jarring song
Of the immortal throng,
Sung to the praise of Him
Who is at once its leader and its theme,
My Christ, my King, my God!   BONAR.

"I'm Old To-day!"

I WAKE at last; I've dreamed too long:
  Where are my threescore years and ten?
My eye is keen, my limbs are strong,
  I well might vie with younger men.
The world, its passions and its strife,
  Is passing from my grasp away;
And though this pulse seems full of life,
  I'm old to-day, I'm old to-day!

"Strange that I never felt before
 That I had almost reached my goal!
My bark is nearing death's dark shore;
 Life's waters far behind me roll:
And yet I love their murmuring swell,
 Their distant breakers' proud array;
And must I, can I, say 'Farewell'?
 I'm old to-day, I'm old to-day!

"This house is mine, and those broad lands
 That slumber 'neath yon fervid sky;
Yon brooklet, leaping o'er the sands,
 Hath often met my boyish eye.
I loved those mountains when a child;
 They still look young in green array,
Ye rocky cliffs, ye summits wild,
 I'm old to-day, I'm old to-day!

"'Twixt yesterday's short hours and me
 A mighty gulf has intervened;
A man with men I seemed to be;
 But now 't is meet I should be weaned
From all my kind, my kindred dear,
 From those deep skies, that landscape gay,
From joys and hopes I've cherished here;
 I'm old to-day, I'm old to-day!"

O man of years! while earth recedes,
 Look forward, upward, not behind!
Why dost thou lean on broken reeds?
 Why still with earthly fetters bind

Thine ardent soul? God gave it wings
'Mid higher, purer joys to stray !
In heaven no happy spirit sings,
"I'm old to-day, I'm old to-day !"

Old Age.

IS it an evil to be drawing near
   The time when I shall know as I am known?
Is it an evil that the sky grows clear,
   That sunset light upon my path is thrown,
That truth grows fairer, that temptations cease,
And that I see, afar, a path that leads to peace?

Is it not joy to feel the lapsing years
   Calm down one's spirit? As at eventide
After long storm the far horizon clears,
   The skies shine golden and the stars subside ;
Stern outlines softened in the sunlit air,
And still, as day declines, the restful earth grows fair

And so I drop the roses from my hand,
   And let the thorn-pricks heal, and take my way
Down-hill, across a fair and peaceful land
   Lapped in the golden calm of dying day ;
Glad that the night is near, and glad to know
That, rough or smooth the way, I have not far to go

My Mother!

I NEVER call that gentle name,
  My mother! but I am again
E'en as a child; the very same
  That prattled at thy knee; and fain
Would I forget, in momentary joy,
That I no more can be thy happy boy;

 · Thine artless boy, to whom thy smile
  Was sunshine, and thy frown sad night,
(Though rare that frown, and brief the while
  It veiled from me thy loving light;)
For well-conned task, ambition's highest bliss
To win from thy approving lips a kiss.

I've lived through foreign lands to roam,
  And gazed on many a classic scene;
But oft the thought of that dear home,
  Which once was ours, would intervene,
And bid me close again my languid eye,
To think of thee and those sweet days gone by.

I've pored o'er many a yellow page
  Of ancient wisdom, and have won
Perchance a scholar's name; yet sage
  Or poet ne'er have taught thy son
Lessons so pure, so fraught with holy truth,
As those his mother's faith shed o'er his youth.

If e'er through grace my God shall own
  The offerings of my life and love.

Methinks, when bending close before his throne,
  Amid the ransomed hosts above,
Thy name on my rejoicing lips shall be,
And I will bless that grace for heaven and thee!

For thee and heaven; for thou didst tread
  The way that leads to that blest land,
My often wayward footsteps led
  By thy kind words and patient hand;
And when I wandered far, thy faithful call
Restored my soul from sin's deceitful thrall.

  *   *   *   *   *   *

Mother, thy name is widow; well
  I know no love of mine can fill
The waste place of thy heart, nor dwell
  Within one sacred recess; still
Lean on the faithful bosom of thy son,
My parent! thou art more—my *only* one!

BETHUNE

------◆------

A Daughter's Wish.

MY mother!
  It sometimes strengthens me for care,
    And quells a mental strife,
  To think how quietly you bore
    The various ills of life!
  Would that your daughter had a tithe
    Of what you once possessed—
  The calm forbearing gentleness
    That filled her mother's breast!

The Aged Mother.

IS she not beautiful,
    Graceful, and fair,
    In her armchair,
So cheerful and dutiful,
    Sitting, sitting,
    Knitting, knitting,
With ivory needles, her strips so long,
Woven together with chat and song,
Her rainbow matting to lay on the floor
For the feet she loves, by the chair or door?
    Sitting, sitting,
    Knitting, knitting,
Never a murmur from day to day,
Happily passing her life away.
As blessed as a child in its sportive glee
Is our dear mother at eighty-three.

    We call her beautiful
        As she sits there
        In her armchair,
Her snow-white cap o'er her snow-white hair,
Her 'kerchief, pure as a lily's crest,
Smoothly folded upon her breast,
Smooth and clear as her life of rest:
Her robe and shawl, of a twilight gray,
Falling in softened folds away
From her busy hands as she is sit'ing,
Busily reading or busily knitting.

From morn till night,
Cloudy or bright,
Ever contented and blessed is she,
Our dear mother at eighty-three.

Oh, maidens fair, with shining hair,
And cheeks and lips like strawberry-tips,
With springing feet that upward still
Essay to gain life's summit hill ;
Oh think, before you reach the height,
To gather jewels by the way,
As now you may
On left and right,
For strewn beside your path they lay —
The pearls of faith for ever pure,
Diamonds of hope for ever bright,
And charity's sweet gems of light,
That will endure,
And weave a crown so beautiful,
Filled in with loves so dutiful,
That when you come to totter down
"The other side," your lives may be
A benediction, as to me
Is our blest mother's at eighty-three.

MRS. CA

A Wife's Counsel.

COME near me, wife; I fare the better far
For the sweet food of thy divine advice.
Let no man value at a little price
A virtuous woman's counsel: her winged spirit
Is feathered oftentimes with heavenly words,
And like her beauty, ravishing and pure.

CHAPMAN.

The Silver Wedding.

THE shell that once has learned to sing
    The sweet song of the sea,
Never forgets the soughing notes
    Of that deep symphony;
But ever from its winding throat
    The lingering music sighs,
Soft as an angel's breath, that bears
    Celestial harmonies.

Thus through the spiral of the years
    As voices breathe from shells,
There come sweet notes of joy to-day
    From distant marriage bells;
Sweet marriage bells, dear marriage bells
    That touch a chord so live,
It vibrates just as thrillingly
    Through circles twenty-five.

And, chiming with those marriage bells,
    Whose tones wind to us here,
Sweet infant voices, childhood's song,
    Salute your SILVER year.

Oh, may this coil of wedded years
    Still wind and wind away,
Until this silvery song becomes
    A golden roundelay !
May this blest flagon ne'er be drained,
    This wine of life drunk up,
Until, in twenty-five years more,
    It fills a GOLDEN cup.

A Mother's Place.

NO earthly friend a mother's place can fill !
    There is an instinct love, an added sense
Within a mother's breast, that draweth thence
Rare quickness of perception, to discern
Her offspring's wants.   She needeth not to learn
By voice or gesture.   Swift her footsteps glide,
Noiseless as Silence' self; and at the side
Of her beloved one, with love's strength inspired,
She is content to watch for hours untired—
To move the weary limb, and soft recline
The aching head ; the language of a sign,
Wishes unshaped in words, by glance or sigh,
Quick to interpret and to gratify.

Grandmother.

JUST as the sun rose blushing red
Over the hill tops, somebody said,
In broken accents of mourning woe,
Sobbing aloud, but sobbing low:
"Grandmother is dead!"

When the sorrowful murmur broke,
Out from our beautiful dreams we woke,
Feeling a sense of terrible loss;
"She was gold, refined from its dross,"
So somebody spoke.

Just as she sometimes sat in her chair,
Lifting her heart in silent prayer,
Looked she; only a purple mist
Her drooping lids and thin lips kissed,
And rested there.

Only yesterday, how she planned
Labors of love for her aged hand:
"Whenever my useful days are o'er
Let me go to the heavenly shore,"
Was her demand.

Dear old grandmother! How her prayer
Quickened the ear of Eternal care!
And, with only a warning pain,
His angel gathered her soul again
To those regions fair.

Blessed is it for her to sleep :
Can it be wrong for us to weep ?—
We who loved her so well and knew
All the worth of her loving, too,
    And her wisdom deep.

She was aged and knew the way
Youthful feet were inclined to stray:
"The young are giddy, and they must learn
Of hard experience ere they turn,"
    She would gently say.

Happy grandmother ! Would that we
Might share with you the mystery
Of that Beyond, where a thought of sin
Never, oh ! never can enter in,
    Through eternity.

A Mother Showing the Portrait of her Child.

L IVING child or pictured cherub
   Ne'er o'ermatched its baby grace ;
  And the mother, moving nearer,
    Looked it calmly in the face ;
  Then with slight and quiet gesture,
    And with lips that scarcely smiled,
  Said, "A portrait of my daughter
    When she was a child !"

Easy thought was hers to fathom,
  Nothing hard her glance to read,
For it seemed to say, "No praises
  For this little child I need ;
If you see, I see far better,
  And I will not feign to care
For a stranger's prompt assurance
  That the face is fair."   JEAN INGELOW.

Written in a Son's Bible.

REMEMBER, love, who gave thee this,
  When other days shall come,
When she who had thy earliest kiss
  Sleeps in her narrow home :
Remember 't was a mother gave
The gift to one she 'd die to save.

That mother sought a pledge of love,
  The holiest, for her son ;
And from the gifts of God above
  She chose a goodly one :
She chose, for her beloved boy,
The source of life and light and joy ;

And bade him keep the gift, that when
  The parting hour should come,
They might have hope to meet again
  In her eternal home :
She said his faith in that should be
Sweet incense to her memory.

And should the scoffer in his pride
  Laugh that fond gift to scorn,
And bid him cast that gift aside
  That he from youth had borne,
She bade him pause, and ask his breast
If he or she had loved him best.

A parent's blessing on her son
  Goes with this holy thing ;
The love that would retain the one,
  Must to the other cling :
Remember, 't is no idle toy,
A MOTHER'S GIFT—REMEMBER, BOY'!

Sweetest Words!

SOME precious words are born of earth ;
  Some others by the angels given ;
But sweetest of celestial birth,
  Are these: "My Mother," "Home," and "Heaven."

Our Mother's Death.

SILENTLY over land and sea
  Came down the winter's night
Bearing upon its ebon wings
  A mantle purely white,

A spangled robe, as beautiful
As the immortals wear ;
And over all the land it spread
The vesture soft and fair.

Over the frozen river's breast,
And o'er the town 't was spread,
And o'er the monuments and mounds
Above the quiet dead.

Within our peaceful, sheltered home,
Where all was bright and warm,
Was one preparing to go forth,
But not into the storm.

We gathered round our mother's bed
To catch her parting breath ;
But one stood nearer to her heart ;
We knew his name was—Death !

And from our love and from our grief,
And from our dwelling warm,
He bore our mother in his arms,
But not into the storm.

She went unseen—but not alone,
Dear pilgrim of the earth ;
For Jesus took her by the hand,
And gently bore her forth.

And the sweet word she left for us
Shall our life's watchword be :
"As I have followed Jesus' steps,
Beloved ones, follow me !"

We laid her body down to sleep
  Where all is sweet and still, .
Where the last rays of sunlight fall
  Upon the westward hill.

And precious, precious to our hearts
  Shall be that sacred spot ;
While by the Lord she loved so well
  It will not be forgot.

Wasted and wan, we laid her down,
  Worn out with mortal strife ;
But fair and glorious shall she rise
  To glad eternal life.

O heavenly Father, teach us how
  To live, and how to die,
That we may with our mother rise
  To IMMORTALITY !   AUGUSTA MOORE.

---◆---

In Memoriam.

WHAT did we ask, with all our love for him,
  But just a little breath of fuller life,
To float the laboring lungs?   And God hath given
Him life itself—full, everlasting life !
What did we pray for?   Rest, even for a night,
That he might rise with sleep's most golden dews
Refreshed, to feel the morning in his soul ;
And God hath given him His eternal rest.

We could not offer freedom for one hour
From that dread weight of weariness they bear
Who try for years to shake death's shadow off;
And God hath made him free for evermore!

Before me hangs his picture on the wall,
Alive still with the loving, cordial eyes.
How tenderly their winsome lustre laughed!
The fine pale face, pathetically sweet,
So thin with suffering that it seemed a soul;
We feared the angels might be kissing it
Too often and too wooingly for us;
The hands, so woman-white and delicate,
That day by day were gliding from our grasp,
They used to make my heart ache many a time.

I see another picture now: the form
Ye sowed in weakness hath been raised in power –
A pleasure-palace for a prison of pain!
The beauty of his nature that we felt,
Is featured in the shape he weareth now;
The same kind face, but changed and glorified.
From life's unclouded summit it looks back,
And sweetly smiles at all the sorrows past,
With such a look as taketh away grief;
No longer pale, and there is no more pain.
His face is rosed with heaven's immortal bloom,
For he hath found the land of health at last,
The one Physician who can cure all ills;
And he hath eaten of the tree of life,
And felt the eternal spring!   GERALD MASSEY

Now and Hereafter.

"TWO HANDS UPON THE BREAST, AND LABOR IS PAST."
Russian Proverb

TWO hands upon the breast,
    And labor's done ;
Two pale feet crossed in rest—
    The race is run !
Two eyes with coin-weights shut,
    And all tears cease ;
Two lips where grief is mute,
    And wrath at peace !"
So pray we oftentimes, mourning our lot ;
God in his kindness answereth not.

"Two hands to work addrest
    Aye for His praise ;
Two feet that never rest,
    Walking His ways ;
Two eyes that look above,
    Still through all tears ;
Two lips that breathe but love,
    Nevermore fears."
So cry we afterwards, low at our knees.
Pardon those erring prayers, Father ! hear these.

MISS MULOCK.

Finish Thy Work.

FINISH thy work ; the time is short,
　　The sun is in the west,
The night is coming down ; till then
　　Think not of rest.

Yes, finish *all* thy work, then rest ;
　　Till then, rest never :
The rest prepared for thee by God
　　Is rest for ever.

Finish thy work ; then wipe thy brow,
　　Ungird thee from thy toil ;
Take breath, and from each weary limb
　　Shake off the soil.

Finish thy work : then sit thee down
　　On some celestial hill,
And of its strength-reviving air
　　Take thou thy fill.

Finish thy work ; then go in peace,
　　Life's battle fought and won ;
Hear from the Master's throne his voice·
　　"Well done, well done !"

Finish thy work ; then take thy harp,
　　Give praise to God above ;
Sing a new song of endless joy
　　And heavenly love.

Give thanks to Him who held thee up
In all thy path below,
Who made thee faithful unto death,
And crowns thee now.　　　　E. S. MILLER.

There's Crape on the Door.

SOME one has gone from this strange world of ours,
No more to gather its thorns with its flowers ;
No more to linger where sunbeams must fade,
Where on all beauty death's fingers are laid ;
Weary with mingling life's bitter and sweet,
Weary with parting, never to meet ;
Gone, we will hope, to the bright golden shore.
Ring the bell softly, there 's crape on the door !
Ring the bell *sofily*, there 's crape on the door !

Some one is resting from sorrow and sin,
Happy where earthly strifes enter not in ;
Joyous as birds when the morning is bright,
And the sweet sunbeams have bro't us their light.
Weary with sowing and never to reap,
Weary with labor and welcoming sleep ;
Some one 's departed for heaven's bright shore,
Ring the bell softly, there 's crape on the door !
Ring the bell *sofily*, there 's crape on the door !

Angels were anxiously longing to meet
One who walks with them in heaven's bright street ;

Loved ones have whispered that some one is blest,
Free from earth's trials and taking sweet rest.
Yes, there is one more in heavenly bliss,
One less to cherish, and one less to kiss ;
One more departed for heaven's bright shore.
Ring the bell softly, there's crape on the door !
Ring the bell *softly*, there's crape on the door !

"Poor Ellen."

'TIS *hard* to die in spring-time,
    When, to mock my bitter need,
All life around runs over
    In its fulness without heed :
New life for tiniest twig on tree,
New worlds of honey for the bee,
And not one drop of dew for me,
    Who perish as I plead !
*   *   *   *   *
'T is *sweet* to die in spring-time,
    For I feel my golden year
Of summer-time eternal
    Is beginning even here !
"Poor Ellen !" now you say and sigh ;
"Poor Ellen !" but to-morrow I
Shall say, "Poor mother !" and on high
    Watch you, and wait you there.

" Follow Me."

THE Master's voice was sweet :
  "I gave my life for thee ;
Bear thou this cross through pain and loss ;
  Arise and follow me."
I clasped it in my hands :
  "O Thou who diedst for me,
The day is bright, my step is light,
  'T is sweet to follow thee !"

Through the long summer day
  I followed lovingly ;
'T was bliss to hear his voice so near,
  His glorious face to see.
Down where the lilies pale
  Fringed the bright river's brim,
In pastures green his steps were seen—
  'T was sweet to follow him.

Oh, sweet to follow him !
  "Lord, let us here abide."
The flowers were fair, I lingered there,
  I laid his cross aside.
I saw his face no more
  By that bright river's brim ;
Before me lay the desert way—
  'T was hard to follow him.

Yes, hard to follow him
  Into that dreary land :
I was alone ; his cross had grown
  Too heavy for my hand.
I heard his voice afar
  Sound through the night air chill ;
My weary feet refused to meet
  His coming o'er the hill.

The Master's voice was sad :
  "I gave my life for thee ;
I bore the cross through pain and loss ;
  Thou hast not followed me."
"So fair the lilied banks,
  So bleak the desert way ;
The night was dark, I could not mark
  Where thy blest footsteps lay."

"Fairer the lilied banks,
  Softer the grassy lea,
The endless rest of those who best
  Have learned to follow me.
Canst thou not follow me,
  All weary as thou art ?
Hath patient love no power to move
  Thy slow and faithless heart ?
Wilt thou not follow me ?
  These weary feet of mine
Have stained red the pathway dread
  For thee and thine."

"O Lord, O Love divine,
　Once more I follow thee !
Let me abide so near thy side,
　That I thy face may see.
I clasp thy piercéd hand,
　O thou that diedst for me ;
I 'll bear thy cross through pain and loss,
　So I may cling to thee."

———◆———

Trust.

I KNOW not if or dark or bright
　　Shall be my lot ;
　If that wherein my hopes delight
　　Be blest or not.

　It may be mine to drag for years
　　Toil 's heavy chain ;
　Or, day and night, my meat be tears
　　On bed of pain.

　Dear faces may surround my hearth
　　With smiles and glee ;
　Or I may dwell alone, and mirth
　　Be strange to me.

　My bark is wafted from the strand
　　By breath divine,
　And on the helm there rests a hand
　　Other than mine.

One, who has known in storms to sail,
  I have on board ;
Above the raging of the gale
  I hear my Lord.

He holds me when the billows smite ;
  I shall not fall.
If sharp, 't is short ; if long, 't is light ·
  He tempers all.

Safe to the land ! safe to the land !
  The end is this !
And then with him go hand in hand
  Far into bliss.

Evening Hymn.

SUN of my soul, thou Saviour dear,
  It is not night if thou be near ;
  Oh ! may no earth-born cloud arise
  To hide thee from thy servant's eyes !

When the soft dews of kindly sleep
My wearied eyelids gently steep,
Be my last thought : How sweet to rest
For ever on my Saviour's breast !

Abide with me from morn till eve,
For without thee I cannot live !
Abide with me when night is nigh,
For without thee I dare not die.

Thou framer of the light and dark,
Steer through the tempest thine own ark !
Amid the howling, mighty sea,
We are in port if we have thee.

Oh ! by thine own sad burthen, borne
So meekly up the hill of scorn,
Teach thou thy priests their daily cross,
To bear as thine, nor count it loss !

If some poor wandering child of thine
Have spurned to-day the voice divine ;
Now, Lord, the gracious work begin ;
Let him no more lie down in sin !

Watch by the sick—enrich the poor
With blessings from thy boundless store !
Be every mourner's sleep to-night
Like infant's slumber, pure and light !

Come near and bless us when we wake,
Ere through the world our way we take,
Till, in the ocean of thy love,
We lose ourselves in heaven above !   KEBLE.

—————•—————

Night Thought.

IN silence of the voiceless night,
When chased by dreams the slumbers flee,
Whom in the darkness do I seek,
    O God, but thee?

And if there weigh upon my breast
Vague memories of the day foregone,
Scarce knowing why, I fly to thee,
        And lay them down.

Or if it be the gloom that comes
In dread of an impending ill,
My bosom heeds not what it is,
        Since 't is thy will.

For oh ! in spite of constant care,
Or aught beside, how joyfully
I pass that solitary hour,
        My God, with thee.

More tranquil than the stilly night,
More peaceful than that voiceless hour,
Supremely blest, my bosom lies
        Beneath thy power.

For what on earth can I desire
Of all it hath to offer me ?
Or whom in heaven do I seek,
        O God, but thee ?

----•----

The Golden Mile-Stone.

EACH man's chimney is his golden mile-stone ;
    Is the central point from which he measures
        Every distance
Through the gateways of the world around him.

In his farthest wanderings still he sees it ;
Hears the talking flame, the answering night-wind,
      As he heard them
When he sat with those who were, but are not.

Happy he whom neither wealth nor fashion,
Nor the march of the encroaching city,
      Drives an exile
From the hearth of his ancestral homestead.

We may build more splendid habitations,
Fill our rooms with paintings and with sculptures,
      But we cannot
Buy with gold the old associations !

LONGFELLOW.

Be Patient.

BE patient ! oh, be patient ! Put your ear against the
     earth ;
Listen there how noiselessly the germ o' the seed
     has birth—
How noiselessly and gently it upheaves its little way,
'Till it parts the scarcely broken ground and the
     blade stands up in the day.

Be patient ! oh, be patient ! go and watch the wheat
     ears grow—
So imperceptibly that ye can mark nor change nor
     throe—

Day after day, day after day, till the ear is fully
  grown,
And then again day after day, till the ripened field is
  brown.   TRENCH

Evening Prayer.

GOD, that madest earth and heaven,
      Darkness and light!
Who the day for toil hast given,
      For rest the night;
May thine angel guards defend us,
Slumber sweet thy mercy send us,
Holy dreams and hopes attend us,
      This livelong night!   HEBER.

"Do You Think of Me as I Think of You?"

"DO you think of me as I think of you,
    My friends, my friends?" She said it on the sea,
The English minstrel in her minstrelsy,
While under brighter skies than erst she knew
Her heart grew dark, and groped there as the
      blind
To reach, across the waves, friends left behind:
"Do you think of me as I think of you?"

It seemed not much to ask, "As I of you?"
We all do ask the same; no eyelids cover
Within the meekest eyes that question over:
And little in this world the loving do
But sit (among the rocks?) and listen for
The echo of their own love evermore:
"Do you think of me as I think of you?"

"Do you think of me as I think of you?"
O friends, O kindred, O dear brotherhood
Of all the world! What are we that we should
For covenants of long affection sue?
Why press so near each other when the touch
Is barred by graves? Not much and yet too
    much
Is this, "Think of me as I think of you!"

But while on mortal lips I shape anew
A sigh to mortal issues, verily
Above the unshaken stars, that see us die,
A vocal pathos rolls! and He who drew
All life from dust, and for all tasted death,
By death, and life, and love, appealing saith—
"*Do you think of* ME *as I think of you?*"

MRS. BROWNING.

The Silent Hour.

SILENTLY the shades of evening
    Gather round my lowly door;
Silently they bring before me
    Faces I shall see no more.

Oh, the lost, the unforgotten!
Though the world be oft forgot;
Oh, the shrouded and the lonely—
In our hearts they perish not.

Living in the silent hours
Where our spirits only blend,
They unlinked with earthly trouble,
We still hoping for its end.

How such holy memories cluster,
Like the stars when storms are past
Pointing up to that far heaven
We may hope to gain at last.

———•———

"The Lord will Provide."

IN some way or other the Lord will provide:
It may not be *my* way,
It may not be *thy* way;
And yet in his *own* way
"The Lord will provide."

At some time or other the Lord will provide:
It may not be *my* time,
It may not be *thy* time;
And yet in his *own* time
"The Lord will provide."

Despond then no longer, "the Lord will provide:"
  And this be the token,
  No word he hath spoken
  Was ever yet broken—
  "The Lord will provide."

March on then right boldly, the sea shall divide:
  Thy pathway made glorious,
  With shoutings victorious
  We 'll join in the chorus,
  "The Lord will provide!"

MRS. M. A. W. COOKE.

A Flower.

GOD wills but ill," the doubter said,
  "Lo, time doth evil only bear;
Give me a sign His love to prove—
  His vaunted goodness to declare!"

The poet paused by where a flower,
  A simple daisy, starred the sod,
And answered, "Proof of love and power,
  Behold! behold a smile of God!"

BENNETT.

Little White Lily.

LITTLE white lily sat by a stone,
  Drooping and waiting till the sun shone,
Little white lily sunshine has fed;
Little white lily is lifting her head.

Little white lily said, "It is good—
Little white lily's clothing and food :"
Little white lily dressed like a bride,
Shining with whiteness and crowned beside!

Little white lily droopeth with pain,
Watching and waiting for the wet rain.
Little white lily holdeth her cup ;
Rain is fast falling and filling it up.

Little white lily said, "Good again,
When I am thirsty to have nice rain ;
Now I am stronger, now I am cool ;
Heat cannot burn me, my veins are so full."

Little white lily smells very sweet,
On her head sunshine, rain at her feet :
"Thanks to the sunshine, thanks to the rain !
Little white lily is happy again !"   G. M'DCNALD.

Lesson of the Flowers.

EVERY flower is sweet to me :
    The rose and violet,
The pink, the daisy, and sweet pea,
    Heart's-ease and mignonette,
And hyacinths and daffodillies ;
But sweetest are the spotless lilies.

I know not what the lilies were
    That grew in ancient times—
When Jesus walked with children fair
    Through groves of eastern climes,
And made each flower as He passed by it,
A type of faith, content, and quiet.

But they were not more pure and bright
    Than those our gardens show,
Or those that shed their silver light
    Where the dark waters flow,
Or those that hide in woodland alley
The fragrant lilies of the valley.

And I in each of them can see
    Some lesson for my youth:
The loveliness of purity,
    The stateliness of truth,
Whene'er I look upon the lustre
Of those that in the garden cluster.

Patience and hope that keep the soul
    Unruffled and secure,
Though floods of grief beneath it roll,
    I learn, when calm and pure
I see the floating water-lily,
Gleam amid shadows dark and chilly.

And when the fragrance that ascends,
    Shows where its lovely face

The lily of the valley bends,
   I think of that sweet grace,
Which sheds within the spirit lowly,
   A rest, like heaven's, so safe and holy.

CAROLINE MAY.

A Pressed Flower.

A PRESSED flower I love,
   Not for itself—but that its form is linked
With things departed
And with days gone by !

Green Things Growing.

OH ! the green things growing ! the green things grow-
   ing,
The fresh sweet smell of the green things growing,
I would like to live, whether I laugh or grieve,
To watch the happy life of the green things growing.

Oh, the fluttering and pattering of the green things
   growing,
Talking each to each when no man is knowing,
In the wonderful white of the weird moonlight,
Or the gray dreamy dawn when the cocks are crowing.

I love, I love them so, the green things growing,
And I think that they love me without false showing,
For by many a tender touch they comfort me so much,
With the mute, mute comfort of green things growing.

And in the full wealth of their blossoms glowing,
Ten for one I take they 're on me bestowing,
Ah, I should like to see, if God's will it might be,
Many, many a summer of my green things growing.

MISS MULOCK.

"And We shall all be Changed."

YE dainty mosses, lichens gray,
  Pressed each to each in tender fold,
And peacefully thus, day by day,
  Returning to the mould ;

Brown leaves that with aerial grace
  Slip from your branch like birds a-wing,
Each leaving in its appointed place
  A bud of future spring ;

If we, God's conscious creatures, knew
  But half your faith, in our decay,
We should not tremble as we do
  When summoned clay to clay.

But with an equal patience sweet
  We should put off this mortal gear,
In whatsoe'er new form is meet
  Content to reappear.

Knowing each germ of life he gives
  Must have in him its source and rise ;
Being that of his being lives
  May change, but never dies.

Ye dead leaves, dropping soft and slow,
  Ye mosses green, and lichens fair,
Go to your graves, as I will go,
  For God is also there !

MISS MULOCK.

----●----

The Best in Store.

MY God, I thank Thee who hast made
    The earth so bright—
So full of splendor and of joy,
    Beauty and light :
So many glorious things are here
    Noble and right !

I thank Thee, too, that thou hast made
    Joy to abound :
So many gentle thoughts and deeds
    Circling us round,
That in the darkest spot of earth
    Some love is found.

I thank Thee more that all our joy
    Is touched with pain ;
That shadows fall in brightest homes ;
    That thorns remain :
So that earth's bliss may be our guide
    And not our chain.

For thou who knowest, Lord, how soon
  Our weak heart clings,
Hast given us joys tender and true
  Yet all with wings:
So that we see gleaming on high,
  Diviner things!

I thank thee, Lord, that thou hast kept
  The best in store.
We have enough, yet not too much
  To long for more,
A yearning for a deeper peace
  Not known before.

I thank thee, Lord, that here our souls
  Though amply blest,
Can never find, although they seek,
  A perfect rest:
Nor ever shall, until they lean
  On Jesus' breast.

The Humble Heart.

THY home is with the humble, Lord!
  The simplest are the best;
Thy lodging is in child-like hearts;
  Thou makest there thy rest.

Dear Comforter ! Eternal Love !
    If thou wilt stay with me,
Of lowly thoughts and simple ways
    I 'll build a house for thee.

Who made this beating heart of mine
    But thou, my heavenly Guest?
Let no one have it, then, but thee,
    And let it be thy rest.   LYRA CATH

My Cross of Moss.

A TINY cross
    Of soft wood moss,
        And that is all !
And yet it hath a voice, and speaks to me
Of patient faith and holy victory ;
Faith that could triumph in Gethsemane,
And for our sins a sinless sufferer be
        Upon the cross.

A shadowy cross,
    Of soft gray moss !
        And that is all !
But when from sinful thoughts I fain would flee,
This little cross reproaches silently,
As if it said, "Canst thou ungrateful be,
When Christ, to cleanse from sin, hath died for thee
        Nailed to the cross?"

A little cross
Of velvet moss,
And that is all !
Yet when I 've left my darlings with the dead,
And storms of sorrow have swept o'er my head,
I 've seen his beacon cross thro' tears and said—
"What grief he bore !   I will be comforted,
And bear my cross."

Oh, tiny cross,
Of forest moss !
That is not all !
I 'll have thee for my daily guard and guide,
And learn of thee to conquer sin and pride !
Thou shalt speak oft of Jesus crucified,
And all the burden of life's woes I 'll hide
Beneath His cross.

The Hour of Prayer.

MY God, is any hour so sweet,
      From blush of morn to evening star,
As that which calls me to thy feet,
      The calm and holy hour of prayer ?

Blest is the tranquil break of morn,
      And blest the hush of solemn eve,
When on the wings of prayer upborne,
      This fair but transient world I leave.

Then is my strength by thee renewed ;
Then are my sins by thee forgiven :
Then dost thou cheer my solitude
   With clear and beauteous hopes of heaven.

No words can tell what sweet relief
   There for my every want I find ;
What strength for warfare, balm for grief,
   What deep and cheerful peace of mind.

Lord, till I reach that blissful shore,
   No privilege so dear shall be,
As thus my inmost soul to pour
   In faithful filial prayer to thee.

Prayer.

A PRAYER that is said alone
  Starves, having no companion.
Great things ask for, when thou dost pray ;
And those great are which ne'er decay.
Pray not for silver—rust eats this ;
Ask not for gold, which metal is ;
Nor yet for houses, which are here
But earth ; such prayers ne'er reach God's ear.

                        HERRICK

"Let not Your Heart be Troubled."

HE will smile on thee.
  One smile of his shall be enough to heal,
The wound of man's neglect; and he will sigh,
Pitying the trouble which that sigh shall cure;
And he will speak—speak in the desolate night,
In the dark night: "For me a thorny crown
Men wove, and nails were driven in my hands
And feet: there was an earthquake, and I died—
I died, and am alive for evermore!
I died for thee; for thee I am alive,
And my humanity doth mourn with thee,
For thou art mine; and all thy little ones,
They, too, are mine, are mine.

              "Behold, the house
Is dark; but there is brightness where the sons
Of God are singing; and behold, the heart
Is troubled; yet the nations walk in white;
They have forgotten how to weep: and thou
Shalt also come, and I will foster thee
And satisfy thy soul; and thou shalt warm
Thy trembling life beneath the smile of God!
A little while—it is a little while—
A little while, and I will comfort thee:
I go away, but I will come again."

A Sick-Bed.

LONG hast thou watched my bed,
　　And smoothed the pillow oft
For this poor aching head,
　　With touches kind and soft.

Oh, smooth it yet again,
　　As softly as before ;
Once, only once, and then
　　I need thy hand no more.

Yet here I may not stay,
　　Where I so long have lain,
Through many a restless day
　　And many a night of pain.

But bear me gently forth
　　Beneath the open sky,
Where, on the pleasant earth,
　　Till night the sunbeams lie.

There, through the coming days,
　　I shall not look to thee,
My weary side to raise,
　　And shift it tenderly.

There sweetly shall I sleep,
　　Nor wilt thou need to bring
And put to my hot lip
　　Cool water from the spring ;

Nor wet the 'kerchief laid
  Upon my burning brow;
Nor from my eyelids shade
  The light that wounds them now;

Nor watch that none shall tread,
  With noisy footstep, nigh;
Nor listen by my bed
  To hear my faintest sigh;

And feign a look of cheer,
  And words of comfort speak,
Yet turn to hide the tear
  That gathers on thy cheek.

Beside me, where I rest,
  Thy loving hands will set
The flowers I love the best—
  Moss-rose and violet.

Then to the sleep I crave
  Resign me, till I see
The face of Him who gave
  His life for thee and me.

Yet, with the setting sun,
  Come, now and then, at eve,
And think of me as one
  For whom thou shouldst not grieve;

Who, when the kind release
  From sin and suffering came,
Passed to the appointed peace
  In murmuring thy name.

Leave, at my side, a space,
  Where thou shalt come at last,
To find a resting-place
  When many years are past.

               WM. C. BRYANT

Jesus, I am Never Weary.

JESUS, I am never weary,
  When upon this bed of pain ;
If thy presence only cheer me,
  All my loss I count but gain :
      Ever near me—
  Ever near me, Lord, remain !

Dear ones come with fruit and flowers,
  Thus to cheer my heart the while
In these deeply anxious hours :
  Oh, if Jesus only smile !
      Only Jesus
  Can these trembling fears beguile.

All my sins were cast upon thee,
  All my griefs on thee were laid ;
For the blood of thine atonement
  All my utmost debt has paid :
      Dearest Saviour,
  I believe, for thou hast said.

Dearest Saviour, go not from me,
   Let thy presence still abide;
Look in tenderest love upon me—
   I am sheltered near thy side.
     Dearest Saviour,
   Who for suffering sinners died.

Both mine arms are clasped around thee
   And my head is on thy breast;
For my weary soul has found thee
   Such a *perfect, perfect* rest.
     Dearest Saviour,
   Now I know that I am blest.   MRS. WELLS.

Comfort for Sickness.

OH, how soft that bed must be,
  Made in sickness, Lord, by thee;
And that rest, how calm, how sweet,
Where Jesus and the sufferer meet!

Come, thou good Physician, now,
Soothe my cheek and smooth my brow;
Whisper, raising up my head,
"It is I; be not afraid!"

Bless me, and I shall be blest;
Soothe me, and I shall have rest;
Fix my heart, my hopes above;
Love me, Lord, for thou art Love!

Detained from God's House.

THOUSANDS, O Lord of Hosts, to-day
   Within thy temple meet;
And tens of thousands throng to pay
   Their homage at thy feet.

They sing thy deeds as I have sung,
   In sweet and solemn lays;
Were I among them, my glad tongue
   Might learn new themes of praise.

I may not to thy courts repair,
   Yet here thou surely art:
Oh, give me here a house of prayer;
   Here Sabbath joys impart!

Bearing the Cross.

THE heavier cross, the stronger faith;
   The loaded palm strikes deeper root;
The vine juice sweetly issueth
   When men have pressed the clustered fruit;
And courage grows where dangers come,
Like pearls beneath the salt sea foam.

The heavier cross, the heartier prayer;
   The bruiséd herbs most fragrant are;

If wind and sky were always fair,
  The sailor would not watch the star ;
And David's psalms had ne'er been sung
If David's heart had not been wrung.

Night to the Weary.

FATHER of heaven and earth,
  I bless thee for the night,
  The soft, still night !
  The holy pause of care and mirth,
  Of sound and light !

  Now far in glade and dell,
  Flower-cup and bud and bell
Have shut around the sleeping woodlark's nest ;
  The bee's long murmuring toils are done,
  And I, the o'er-wearied one,
  O'er-wearied and o'er-wrought,
Bless thee, O God, O Father of the oppressed,
  With my last waking thought,
    In the still night !

  Yes, ere I sink to rest,
  By the fire's dying light,
  Thou Lord of earth and heaven,
  I bless thee, who hast given
  Unto life's fainting travellers the night,
  The soft, still, holy night !

"Lovest Thou Me?"

JOHN 21 : 15-17.

L OVEST thou me?" I hear my Saviour say.
Would that my heart had power to answer, "Yea,
Thou knowest all things, Lord, in heaven above
And earth beneath ; thou knowest that I love."
But 't is not so ; in word, in deed, in thought,
I do not, cannot love thee as I ought.
Thy love must give the power, thy love alone ;
There 's nothing worthy of thee but thine own.
Lord, with the love wherewith thou lovest me,
Reflected on thyself, I would love thee.

MONTGOMERY.

"This I did for Thee—What doest Thou for Me?"

MOTTO PLACED UNDER A PRINT OF CHRIST ON THE CROSS.

I GAVE my life for thee,
My precious blood I shed,
That thou might'st ransomed be,
And quickened from the dead.
I gave my life for thee ;
What hast thou given for me?

I spent long years for thee
  In weariness and woe,
That one eternity
  Of joy thou mightest know.
I spent long years for thee :
Hast thou spent *one* for me ?

My Father's house of light,
  My rainbow-circled throne,
I left for earthly night,
  For wanderings sad and lone ;
I left it all for thee ;
Hast thou left aught for me ?

I suffered much for thee,
  More than thy tongue can tell
Of bitterest agony,
  To rescue thee from hell.
I suffered much for thee ;
What dost thou bear for me ?

And I brought down to thee,
  Down from my home above,
Salvation full and free,
  My pardon and my love ;
Great gifts I brought to thee ;
What hast thou brought to me ?

Oh, let thy life be given,
  Thy years for me be spent,

World-fetters all be riven,
  And joy with suffering blent :
Give thou *thyself* to me,
  And I will welcome thee !

Son of the Carpenter.

SON of the carpenter, receive
  This humble work of mine ;
Worth to my meanest labor give,
  By joining it to thine.

Servant of all, to toil for man
  Thou wouldst not, Lord, refuse ;
Thy majesty did not disdain
  To be employed for us.

Thy bright example I pursue,
  To thee in all things rise ;
And all I think, or speak, or do,
  Is but one sacrifice.

Careless through outward cares I go,
  From all distraction free ;
My hands are but engaged below,
  My heart is still with thee.

Oh, when wilt thou, my Life, appear?
  How gladly would I cry :
"'T is done ! the work thou gav'st me here
  'T is finished, Lord !" and fly.

What the Sparrow Chirps.

I AM only a little sparrow,
  A bird of low degree ;
My life is of little value ;
  But the dear Lord cares for me.

He gave me a coat of feathers ;
  It is very plain, I know,
With never a speck of crimson,
  For it was not made for show.

But it keeps me warm in winter,
  And it shields me from the rain ;
Were it bordered with gold or purple,
  Perhaps it would make me vain.

By-and-by, when the spring-time comes,
  I'll build myself a nest,
With many a chirp of pleasure,
  In the spot I like the best.

And He will give me wisdom
  To build it of leaves most brown ;
Soft it must be for my birdies,
  And so I will line it with down.

I have no barn or storehouse,
  I neither sow nor reap ;
God gives me a sparrow's portion,
  But never a seed to keep.

If my meal is sometimes scanty,
    Close picking makes it sweet ;
I have always enough to feed me,
    And "life is more than meat."

I know there are many sparrows—
    All over the world we are found ;
But our heavenly Father knoweth
    When one of us falls to the ground.

Though small, we are never forgotten ;
    Though weak, we are never afraid ;
For we know that the dear Lord keepeth
    The life of the creatures he made.

I fly through the thickest forests,
    I light on many a spray ;
I have no chart nor compass,
    But I never lose my way.

And I fold my wings at twilight,
    Wherever I happen to be ;
For the Father is always watching,
    And no harm will come to me:

I am only a little sparrow,
    A bird of low degree ;
But I know that the Father loves me.
    Have you less faith than we ?

Trust in God.

THE child leans on its parent's breast,
  Leaves there its cares, and is at rest :
The bird sits singing by its nest,
    And tells aloud
His trust in God, and so is blest
    'Neath every cloud.

He hath no store, he sows no seed,
Yet sings aloud, and doth not need ;
By flowing streams or grassy mead,
    He sings to shame
Men, who forget, in fear of need,
    A Father's name.

The heart that trusts, for ever sings,
And feels as light as it had wings ;
A well of peace within it springs ;
    Come good or ill,
Whate'er to-day—to-morrow brings,
    It is His will !

                              ISAAC WILLIAMS.

The Singing Lesson.

A NIGHTINGALE made a mistake ;
  She sang a few notes out of tune :
Her heart was ready to break,
    And she hid away from the moon,

And wrung her claws, poor thing,
  But was far too proud to speak ;
She tucked her head under her wing,
  And pretended to be asleep.

A lark, arm-in-arm with a thrush.
  Came sauntering up to the place ;
The nightingale felt herself blush,
  Though feathers hid her face ;
She knew they had heard her song,
  She felt them snicker and sneer ;
She thought that life was too long,
  And wished she could skip a year.

"O nightingale !" cooed a dove ;
  "O nightingale ! what's the use ?
You bird of beauty and love,
  Why behave like a goose ?
Do n't sulk away from our sight,
  Like a common, contemptible fowl ;
You bird of joy and delight,
  Why behave like an owl ?

"Only think of all you have done ;
  Only think of all you can do ;
A false note is really fun
  From such a bird as you !
Lift up your proud little crest,
  Open your musical beak ;
Other birds have to do their best,
  You need only to speak !"

The nightingale shyly took
  Her head from under her wing,
And, giving the dove a look,
  Straightway began to sing.
There was never a bird that could pass;
  The night was divinely calm;
And the people stood on the grass
  To hear that wonderful psalm!

The nightingale did not care,
  She only sang to the skies;
Her song ascended there,
  And there she fixed her eyes.
The people that stood below
  She knew but little about;
And this tale has a moral, I know,
  If you'll try and find it out!!

JEAN INGELOW.

Humility.

THE bird that soars on highest wing
  Builds on the ground her lowly nest;
And she that doth most sweetly sing,
  Sings in the shade, where all things rest;
In lark and nightingale we see
What honor hath humility.

When Mary chose "the better part,"
  She meekly sat at Jesus' feet;

And Lydia's gently opened heart
    Was made for God's own temple meet:
Fairest and best adorned is she
    Whose clothing is humility.

The saint that wears heaven's brightest crown
    In deepest adoration bends;
The weight of glory bows him down
    Then most, when most his soul ascends.
Nearest the throne itself must be
    The footstool of humility.   MONTGOMERY.

Blessed to Overflowing.

I HAVE enough, O God! my heart to-night
    Runs over with its fulness of content;
And as I look out on the fragrant stars,
And from the beauty of the night take in
My priceless portion—yet myself no more
Than in the universe a grain of sand—
I feel His glory who could make a world,
Yet in the lost depths of the wilderness
Leave not a flower unfinished.

                        Rich, though poor
My low-roofed cottage is this hour a heaven.
Music is in it—and the song she sings,
That sweet-voiced wife of mine, arrests the ear
Of my young child awake upon her knee;

And, with his calm eyes on his master's face,
My noble hound lies couchant ; and all here --
All in this little home, yet boundless heaven--
Are, in such love as I have power to give,
Blesséd to overflowing.

          Thou who look'st
Upon my brimming heart this tranquil eve,
Knowest its fulness, as thou dost the dew
Sent to the hidden violet by thee ;
And as that flower, from its unseen abode,
Sends its sweet breath up, duly, to the sky,
Changing its gift to incense, so, O God,
May the sweet drops that to my humble cup
Find their far way from heaven, send up to Thee
Fragrance at thy throne welcome !   WILLIS.

Why thus Longing?

WHY thus longing, thus for ever sighing
  For the far-off, unattained and dim ;
While the beautiful all round thee lying
  Offers up its low perpetual hymn?

Wouldst thou listen to its gentle teaching
  All thy restless yearning it would still,
Leaf and flower and laden bee are preaching
  Thine own sphere though humble first to fill.

Poor indeed thou must be, if around thee
   Thou no ray of light and joy canst throw;
If no silken cord of love hath bound thee
   To some little world through weal or woe.

If no dear eyes thy fond love can brighten,
   No fond voices answer to thine own;
If no brother's sorrow thou canst lighten
   By tender sympathy and gentle tone.

Not by deeds that win the crowd's applauses;
   Not by works that give thee world-renown;
Not by martyrdom or vaunted crosses,
   Canst thou win and wear the immortal crown.

Daily struggling, though unloved and lonely,
   Every day a rich reward will give;
Thou wilt find by hearty striving only,
   Truly loving thou canst truly live.

MRS. LISZT.

No Act Falls Fruitless.

SCORN not the slightest word or deed,
   Nor deem it void of power;
There's fruit in each wind-wafted seed
   That waits its natal hour.
A whispered word may touch the heart,
   And call it back to life;
A look of love bid sin depart,
   And still unholy strife.

No act falls fruitless ; none can tell
   How vast its power may be,
Nor what results infolded dwell
   Within it silently.
Work on, despair not, bring thy mite,
   Nor care how small it be ;
God is with all that serve the right,
   The holy, true, and free.

The Cruse that Faileth Not.

"THERE IS THAT SCATTERETH, AND YET INCREASETH."

IS thy cruse of comfort wasting?
   Rise and share it with another,
And through all the years of famine
   It shall serve thee and thy brother.

Love divine will fill thy storehouse,
   Or thy handful still renew ;
Scanty fare for one will often
   Make a royal feast for two.

For the heart grows rich in giving ;
   All its wealth is living grain ;
Seeds, which mildew in the garner,
   Scattered, fill with gold the plain.

Is thy burden hard and heavy ?
   Do thy steps drag heavily ?
Help to bear thy brother's burden ;
   God will bear both it and thee.

Numb and weary on the mountains,
　Wouldst thou sleep amid the snow?
Chafe that frozen form beside thee,
　And together both shall glow.

Art thou stricken in life's battles?
　Many wounded round thee moan;
Lavish on their wounds thy balsams,
　And that balm shall heal thine own.

Is thy heart a well left empty?
　None but God its void can fill;
Nothing but a ceaseless fountain
　Can its ceaseless longings fill.

Is thy heart a living power?
　Self-entwined its strength sinks low;
It can only live in loving,
　And by serving, love will grow.

MRS. CHARLES

Speak Gently.

SPEAK gently—it is better far
　To rule by love than fear;
Speak gently, let not harsh words mar
　The good we might do here.

Speak gently—love should whisper low
　To friends when faults we find;
Gently let truthful accents flow,
　Affection's voice is kind.

Speak gently to the little child,
   Its love be sure to gain ;
Teach it in accents soft and mild ;
   It may not long remain.

Speak gently to the young, for they
   Will have enough to bear ;
Pass through this life as best they may,
   'T is full of anxious care.

Speak gently to the aged one,
   Grieve not the careworn heart :
The sands of life are nearly run ;
   Let such in peace depart.

Speak gently, kindly to the poor,
   Let no harsh tone be heard ;
They have enough they must endure
   Without an unkind word.

Speak gently to the erring, know
   That thou art also man ;
Perchance unkindness drove them so :
   Oh win them back again.

Speak gently, for 't is like the Lord,
   Whose accents, meek and mild,
Bespoke him as the Son of God,
   The gracious holy child.

Washed in his blood, redeemed to life,
   The family of heaven
Flee from all anger, wrath and strife,
   Forgive as they 're forgiven.

Heavenly Treasure.

" WHAT I SPENT I HAD ;
WHAT I KEPT I LOST ;
WHAT I GAVE I HAVE!"   OLD EPITAPH.

EVERY coin of earthly treasure
    We have lavished upon earth,
For our simple worldly pleasure,
    May be reckoned something worth ;
For the spending was not losing
    Though the purchase were but small ;
It has perished with the using ;
    We have had it—that is all !

All the gold we leave behind us
    When we turn to dust again,
Though our avarice may blind us,
    We have gathered quite in vain :
Since we neither can direct it,
    By the winds of fortune tossed,
Nor in other worlds expect it,
    What we hoarded we have lost !

But each merciful oblation,
    Seed of pity wisely sown—
What we give in self-negation,
    We may safely call our own ;
For the treasure freely given
    Is the treasure that we hoard,
Since the angels keep, in heaven,
    What is lent unto the Lord !

J. C. S. X .

Sympathy.

THE blessings which the poor and weak can scatter
Have their own season. 'T is a little thing
To give a cup of water; yet its draught
Of cool refreshment, drained by fevered lips,
May give a shock of pleasure to the frame
More exquisite than when nectarean juice
Renews the life of joy in happiest hours.
It is a little thing to speak a phrase
Of common comfort which by daily use
Has almost lost its sense; yet on the ear
Of him who thought to die unmourned 't will fall
Like choicest music; fill the glazing eye
With gentle tears; relax the knotted hand
To know the bonds of fellowship again;
And shed on the departing soul a sense
More precious than the benison of friends
About the honored deathbed of the rich—
To him who else were lonely, that another
Of the great family is near and feels.

TALFOURD.

Over and Over Again.

OVER and over again,
    No matter which way I turn,
I always find in the book of life
    Some lesson I have to learn.

I must take my turn at the mill,
  I must grind out the golden grain,
I must work at my task with a resolute will
  Over and over again.

We cannot measure the need
  Of even the tiniest flower,
Nor check the flow of the golden sands
  That run through a single hour ;
But the morning dews must fall,
  And the sun and the summer rain
Must do their part, and perform it all
  Over and over again.

Over and over again
  The brook through the meadows flows,
And over and over again
  The ponderous mill-wheel goes.
Once doing will not suffice,
  Though doing be not in vain ;
And a blessing failing us once or twice,
  May come if we try again.

The path that has once been trod
  Is never so rough to the feet ;
And the lesson we once have learned
  Is never so hard to repeat.
Though sorrowful tears must fall,
  And the heart to its depths be driven
With storm and tempest, we need them all
  To render us meet for heaven.

M ss JOSEPHINE PO LARD.

Which?

"WHICH shall it be? Which shall it be?"
I looked at John—John looked at me :
Dear patient John, who loves me yet,
As well as though my locks were jet.
And when I found that I must speak,
My voice seemed strangely low and weak :
"Tell me again what Robert said !"
And then I listening bent my head,
"This is his letter :

" 'I will give
A house and land while you shall live,
If, in return, from out your seven,
One child to me for aye is given.' "
I looked at John's old garments worn,
I thought of all that John had borne
Of poverty, and work, and care,
Which I, though willing, could not share ;
I thought of seven mouths to feed,
Of seven little children's need,
And then of this.

"Come, John," said I,
"We 'll choose among them as they lie
Asleep :" so walking hand in hand,
Dear John and I surveyed our band.
First to the cradle light we stepped,
Where Lilian the baby slept,

A glory 'gainst the pillow white.
Softly the father stooped to lay
His rough hand down in loving way,
When dream or whisper made her stir,
And huskily he said : "Not her !"

We stooped beside the trundle-bed,
And one long ray of lamplight shed
Athwart the boyish faces there,
In sleep so pitiful and fair ;
I saw on Jamie's rough red cheek,
A tear undried.   Ere John could speak,
"He's but a baby, too," said I,
And kissed him as we hurried by.

Pale, patient Robbie's angel face
Still in his sleep bore suffering's trace :
"No, for a thousand crowns, not him,"
He whispered, while our eyes were dim.

Poor Dick ! bad Dick ! our wayward son,
Turbulent, reckless, idle one—
Could he be spared?   "Nay, He who gave
Bade us befriend him to the grave ;
Only a mother's heart can be
Patient enough for such as he ;
And so," said John, "I would not dare
To send him from her bedside prayer."

Then stole we softly up above
And knelt by Mary, child of love.

"Perhaps for her 't would better be,"
I said to John.   Quite silently
He lifted up a curl that lay
Across her cheek in wilful way,
And shook his head.   "Nay, love, not thee
The while my heart beat audibly.

Only one more, our eldest lad,
Trusty and truthful, good and glad—
So like his father.   "No, John, no—
I can not, will not let him go."

And so we wrote, in courteous way,
We could not drive one child away.
And afterward, toil lighter seemed,
Thinking of that of which we dreamed,
Happy in truth that not one face
We missed from its accustomed place;
Thankful to work for all the seven,
Trusting the rest to One in heaven!

Mrs. F. L. Beers.

A Little Goosey.

THE chill November day was done,
   The working world home faring,
The wind came roaring through the streets
   And set the gas lamps flaring;
And hopelessly and aimlessly
   The scared old leaves were flying,
When mingled with the sighing wind
   I heard a small voice crying;

And shivering on the corner stood
  A child of four or over;
No cloak nor hat her small soft arms
  And wind-blown curls to cover.
Her dimpled face was stained with tears;
  Her round blue eyes ran over;
She cherished in her wee cold hand
  A bunch of faded clover.

And, one hand round her treasure, while
  She slipped in mine the other,
Half-scared, half-confidential, said,
  "Oh, please I want my mother!"
"Tell me your street and number, pet:
  Don't cry, I'll take you to it."
Sobbing, she answered, "I forget ·
  The organ made me do it.

"He came and played at Milly's steps,
  The monkey took the money,
And so I followed down the street,
  The monkey was so funny;
I've walked about a hundred hours,
  From one street to another;
The monkey's gone, I've spoiled my flowers;
  Oh, please, I want my mother!"

"But, what's your mother's name, and what
  The street? Now think a minute."
"My mother's name is 'Mamma dear';
  The street—I can't begin it."

"But what is strange about the house,
  Or new, not like the others?"
"I guess you mean my trundle-bed,
  Mine and my little brother's.

"Oh, dear! I ought to be at home,
  To help him say his prayers,
He's such a baby, he forgets,
  And we are both such players—
And there's a bar between to keep
  From pitching on each other,
For Harry rolls when he's asleep.
  Oh, dear! I want my mother."

The sky grew stormy; people passed
  All muffled, homeward faring;
"You'll have to spend the night with me,"
  I said at last, despairing.
I tied a kerchief round her neck—
  "What ribbon's this, my blossom?"
"Why, don't you know?" she smiling asked,
  And drew it from her bosom,

A card with number, street, and name!
  My eyes astonished met it;
"For," said the little one, "you see
  I might sometimes forget it;
And so I wear a little thing,
  That tells you all about it;
For mother says she's very sure
  I would get lost without it."

Absence.

WHAT shall I do with all the days and hours
  That must be counted ere I see thy face?
How shall I charm the interval that lowers
  Between this time and that sweet time of grace?

Shall I in slumber steep each weary sense—
  Weary with longing? Shall I flee away
Into past days, and with some fond pretence
  Cheat myself to forget the present day?

Shall love for thee lay on my soul the sin
  Of casting from me God's great gift of time?
Shall I, these mists of memory locked within,
  Leave and forget life's purposes sublime?

Oh how or by what means may I contrive
  To bring the hour that brings thee back more
    near?
How may I teach my drooping hope to live
  Until that blessed time, and thou art here?

I'll tell thee ; for thy sake I will lay hold
  Of all good aims, and consecrate to thee,
In worthy deeds, each moment that is told
  While thou, beloved one! art far from me.

For thee I will arouse my thoughts to try
  All heavenward flights, all high and holy strains;
For thy dear sake I will walk patiently
  Through these long hours, nor call their
    minutes pains.

I will this dreary blank of absence make
A noble task-time, and will therein strive
To follow excellence, and to o'ertake
More good than I have won since yet I live.

So may this doomèd time build up in me
A thousand graces which shall thus be thine :
So may my love and longing hallowed be,
And thy dear thought an influence divine.

MRS. BUTLER.

The Old Man's Comforts.

"YOU are old, father William," the young man cried,
     "The locks which are left you are gray ;
You are hale, father William, a hearty old man ;
     Now tell me the reason, I pray."

"In the days of my youth," father William replied,
     "I remembered that youth would fly fast,
And abused not my health and my vigor at first,
     That I never might need them at last."

"You are old, father William," the young man cried,
     "And pleasures with youth pass away ;
And yet you lament not the days that are gone ;
     Now tell me the reason, I pray."

"In the days of my youth," father William replied,
     "I remembered that youth could not last ;
I thought of the future, whatever I did,
     That I never might grieve for the past."

"You are old, father William," the young man cried,
"And life must be hasting away;
You are cheerful, and love to converse upon death;
Now tell me the reason, I pray."

"I am cheerful, young man," father William replied.
"Let the cause thy attention engage:.
In the days of my youth I remembered my God,
And he hath not forgotten my age."   SOUTHEY.

Age of Children Happiest.

I SAW the little boy,
    In thought how oft that he
Did wish of God to 'scape the rod,
    A tall young man to be.

The young man eke that feels
    His bones with work opprest,
How he would be a rich old man,
    To live and lie at rest.

The rich old man that sees
    His end draw on so sore,
How would he be *a boy* again,
    To live so much the more.

Whereat full oft I smiled
    To see how all those three,
From boy to man, from man to boy,
    Would chop and change degree.

EARL OF SURREY, 16TH CENTURY

Going Home.

WHERE are you going so fast, old man,
　Where are you going so fast?
There's a valley to cross and a river to ford,
There's a clasp of the hand and a parting word,
And a tremulous sigh for the past, old man—
　The beautiful vanished past.

The road has been rugged and rough, old man,
　To your feet it's rugged and rough;
But you see a dear being with gentle eyes
Has shared in your labor and sacrifice.
Ah, that has been sunshine enough, old man,
　For you and me, sunshine enough.

How long since you passed o'er the hill, old man,
　Of life—o'er the top of the hill?
Were there beautiful valleys on t' other side;
Were there flowers and trees, with their branches
　wide,
To shut out the heat of the sun, old man,
　The heat of the fervid sun?

And how did you cross the waves, old man,
　Of sorrow—the fearful waves?
Did you lay your dear treasures by, one by one,
With an aching heart and "God's will be done,'
Under the wayside dust, old man,
　In the graves 'neath the wayside dust?

There is sorrow and labor for all, old man ;
　　Alas, there is sorrow for all ;
And you, peradventure, have had your share,
For eighty long winters have whitened your hair,
And they 've whitened your heart as well, old man.
　　Thank God, your heart as well.

You 're now at the foot of the hill, old man,
　　At last at the foot of the hill ;
The sun has gone down in a golden glow,
And the heavenly city lies just below :
Go in through the pearly gate, old man,
　　The beautiful pearly gate.

I'm Growing Old.

MY days pass pleasantly away,
　　My nights are blessed with sweetest sleep,
I feel no symptoms of decay,
　　I have no cause to mourn or weep ;
My foes are impotent and shy,
　　My friends are neither false nor cold ;
And yet of late I often sigh—
　　　　　　I 'm growing old.

My growing talk of olden times,
　　My growing thirst for early news,
My growing apathy to rhymes,
　　My growing love of easy shoes,

My growing hate of crowds and noise,
My growing fear of catching cold,
All tell me in the plainest voice—
        I 'm growing old !

I 'm growing fonder of my staff,
  I 'm growing dimmer in the eyes,
I 'm growing fainter in my laugh,
  I m growing deeper in my sighs,
I 'm growing careless in my dress,
  I 'm growing frugal of my gold,
I 'm growing wise, I 'm growing—yes,
        I 'm growing old !

I feel it in my changing taste,
  I see it in my changing hair,
I see it in my growing waist,
  I see it in my growing heir ;
A thousand hints proclaim the truth
  As plain as truth was ever told,
That even in my haunted youth—
        I 'm growing old !

Ah me ! my very laurels breathe
  The tale in my reluctant ears ;
And every boon the hours bequeath,
  But makes me debtor to the years ;
E'en Flattery's honeyed words declare
  The secret she would fain withhold,
And tell me in "How young you are !"
        I 'm growing old !

Thanks for the year whose rapid flight
　　My sombre muse too gladly sings ;
Thanks for the gleams of golden light
　　That tint the darkness of their wings;
The light that beams from out the sky,
　　Those heavenly mansions to unfold,
Where all are blest and none shall sigh,
　　　　　　"I'm growing old !"

J. G SAXE.

Towards Evening.

FATHER, the shadows fall
　　Along my way ;
　　'T is past the noon of day ;
My "westering sun" tells that the eve is near ;
　　I know, but feel no fear.
And loved ones have gone home—
　　A holy band.
I hear them call me from the spirit land—
　　A gentle call,
Yes, dear ones, I shall come.

O, not alone ! though now
　　I lead the van,
And with uncovered head
Press on where others led
　　When my young life began.
I am not left alone,
Though they are gone.

Sweet voices of the past,
    And of to-day—
The loved that cheer my way
And twine around my heart,
'Tell me how good thou art.
    O holy light and love!
Beam on my soul,
My inmost life control;
Then may each pure thought spring;
And peace, with gentle wing,
    Brood like the dove.

Rest.

REST is not quitting
    This busy career;
Rest is the fitting
    Of self to one's sphere.

'T is the brook's motion,
    Clear without strife,
Fleeing to the ocean
    After its life.

'T is loving and serving
    The highest and best;
'T is onward, unswerving:
    And this is true rest.   GOETHE.

Three Old Saws.

IF the world seems "cold" to you
  Kindle fires to warm it!
Let their comfort hide from view
  Winters that deform it.
Hearts as frozen as your own
  To that radiance gather ;
You will soon forget to moan
  "Ah! the cheerless weather!"

If the world's a "wilderness,"
  Go build houses in it!
Will it help your loneliness
  On the winds to din it?
Raise a hut, however slight ;
  Weeds and brambles smother,
And to roof and meal invite
  Some forlorner brother.

If the world's "a vale of tears,"
  Smile till rainbows span it!
Breathe the love that life endears ;
  Clear from clouds to fan it.   .
Of your gladness lend a gleam
  Unto souls that shiver ;
Show them how dark sorrow's stream
  Blends with hope's bright river.

The Noble Nature.

IT is not growing like a tree
  In bulk, doth make man better be ;
Or standing long an oak three hundred year,
To fall a log at last, dry, bald, and sere ;
      A lily of a day
      Is fairer far in May,
Although it fall and die that night ;
It was the plant and flower of Light.
In small proportions we just beauty see ;
And in short measures life may perfect be.

BEN JONSON.

As Thou Wilt.

IT is so sweet to live
  My little life to-day
That I would never leave it, if
    I might for ever stay !
    I sometimes say.

I am so weary, Lord,
  I would lie down for aye,
Could I but hear thee speak the word ;
    " Thy sins are washed away !"
    I sometimes say.

The better mood that lies
  These moods between midway,
Comes softly, and I lift my eyes,
  "Lord, as thou wilt!" I pray;
  And would alway.   H. M. KIMBALL.

Little Moments.

LITTLE moments, how they fly,
  Golden-wingéd, flitting by,
Bearing many things for me
Into vast eternity!

Never do they wait to ask,
If completed is my task,
Whether gathering grain or weeds,
Doing good or evil deeds;
Onward haste they evermore,
Adding all unto their store!

And the little moments keep
Record if we wake or sleep,
Of our every thought and deed,
For us all some time to read.

Artists are the moments too,
Ever painting something new,
On the walls and in the air,
Painting pictures everywhere!

If we smile or if we frown,
Little moments put it down,
And the angel, memory,
Guards the whole eternally!

Let us then so careful be,
That they bear for you and me,
On their little noiseless wings
Only good and pleasant things;
And that pictures which they paint
Have no background of complaint:
So the angel, memory,
May not blush for you and me!

The Child on the Judgment-seat.

WHERE hast thou been toiling all day, sweet heart,
    That thy brow is burdened and sad?
The Master's work may make weary feet
    But it leaves the spirit glad.

Was thy garden nipped with the midnight frosts,
    Or scorched with the mid-day glare?
Were thy vines laid low, or thy lilies crushed,
    That thy face is so full of care?

"No pleasant garden-toils were mine,
    I have sat on the judgment-seat,
Where the Master sits at eve, and calls
    The children around his feet."

How camest thou on the judgment-seat,
  Sweet heart, who set thee there?
'T is a lonely and lofty seat for thee,
  And well might fill thee with care.

"I climbed on the judgment-seat myself;
  I have sat there alone all day,
For it grieved me to see the children around
  Idling their life away.

"They wasted the Master's precious seed,
  They wasted the precious hours;
They trained not the vines, nor gathered the fruits,
  And they trampled the sweet meek flowers."

But how fared thy garden-plot, sweet heart,
  Whilst thou sat'st on the judgment-seat?
Who watered thy roses, and trained thy vines
  And kept them from careless feet?

"Nay, that is the saddest of all to me,
  That is saddest of all!
My vines are trailing, my roses are parched,
  My lilies droop and fall."

Go back to thy garden-plot, sweet heart,
  Go back till the evening falls,
And bind thy lilies, and train thy vines,
  Till for thee the Master calls.

Go make thy garden fair as thou canst,
  Thou workest never alone ;
Perchance he whose plot is next to thine
  Will see it and mend his own.

And the next may copy his, sweet heart,
  Till all grows fair and sweet ;
And when the Master comes at eve,
  Happy faces his coming will greet.

Then shall thy joy be full, sweet heart,
  In the garden so fair to see,
In the Master's words of praise to all,
  In a look of his own for thee.   MRS. CHARLES.

Buried To-Day.

BURIED to-day !
  When the soft green buds are bursting out,
  And up on the south wind comes a shout
  Of village boys and girls at play
  In the mild spring evening gray.
   *   *   *   *   *

  Enters to-day
Another body in churchyard sod,
Another soul on the life in God.
Our Christ was buried; and lives alway :
  TRUST HIM, and go your way.   MISS MULOCK.

The Funeral Bell.

FROM the tower,
    Heavy, slow,
  Tolls the funeral
    Bell of woe,
Sad and solemn, with its knell attending
Some new wand'rer on the last way wending.

To mother Earth's dark, silent bosom
    The husbandmen the seed consign,
And hope that it will swell and blossom,
    And bless the sower, by laws divine.
Still costlier seed in sorrow bringing,
    We hide within the lap of earth,
And hope that from the coffin springing,
    'T will bloom in brighter beauty forth.

SCHILLER.

Only a Year Ago.

ONE year—one year—one little year,
    And so much gone !
And yet the even flow of life
    Moves calmly on.

The grave grows green, the flowers bloom fair
    Above that head ;
No sorrowing tint of leaf or spray
    Says he is dead.

No pause or hush of merry birds,
That sing above,
Tells us how coldly sleeps below
The form we love.

Where hast thou been this year, beloved?
What hast thou seen?
What visions fair, what glorious life?
Where hast thou been?

The veil! the veil! so thin, so strong,
Twixt us and thee,
The mystic veil! when shall it fall,
That we may see?

Not dead, not sleeping, not e'en gone,
But present still,
And waiting for the coming hour
Of God's sweet will.

Lord of the living and the dead,
Our Saviour dear,
We lay in silence at thy feet
This sad, sad year.   MRS. STOWE.

Safe.

WRITE it down, angel, in the book,
  Among the lambs of my fair flock.
One more dear name shall be engraved—
  ‘ *By Jesus saved !* ’ ”

The angel paused and wrote it down,
And turned and touched a glowing crown
On which the precious sentence gleamed—
  "By Christ redeemed !"

It was *our* lamb whose name was there,
So precious to our hearts, so fair,
That oft we trembled as he dreamed,
    So near to heaven he seemed.

Ah me ! we would have stayed the hand
Which led him to the beauteous land !
But troops of little ones came down
    To lead him to his crown !

And as he joined the glittering throng,
We almost heard the shout and song
Of countless darlings, gone before
    Unto the shining shore !   c. c. c.

"Not Dead, but Sleepeth."

THE baby wept ;
  The mother took it from the nurse's arms,
And soothed its griefs, and stilled its vain alarms;
    And baby slept.

    Again it weeps,
And God doth take it from the mother's arms,
From present pain and future unknown harms ;
    And baby sleeps !   DR. HINDS.

An Angel in the House.

HOW sweet it were, if without feeble fright,
Or dying of the dreadful beauteous sight,
An angel came to us, and we could bear
To see him issue from the silent air
At evening in our room, and bend on ours
His divine eyes, and bring us from his bowers
News of dear friends, and children who have never
Been dead indeed—as we shall know for ever.
Alas! we think not what we daily see
About our hearths—angels that *are* to be,
Or may be if they will, and we prepare
Their souls and ours to meet in happy air—
A child, a friend, a wife, whose soft heart sings
In unison with ours, breeding its future wings.

L. HUNT.

Taking Flight.

AND she is gone : sweet human love is gone !
'T is only when they spring to heaven, that angels
Reveal themselves to you : they sit all day
Beside you, and lie down at night by you,
Who care not for their presence, muse or sleep—
And all at once they leave you, and you know them.

BROWNING.

Beside the River.

WE stood beside the river
　　Where all our souls must go,
Bearing a loved one in our arms,
Our hearts repeating the alarms
　　That came across the river ;
And saw the sun decline in mist,
That rose until her brow it kissed,
　　And left it cold as snow.

Watching beside the river,
　　With every ebb and flow,
Fond hopes within our hearts would spring,
Until another warning ring
　　Came o'er the fearful river.
We saw the flush, the brightness fade,
The loving lips looked grieved and sad,
　　The white hands whiter grow.

Watching by the river,
　　With anguish none can tell,
And trembling hearts and hands, we strove
To save the darling of our love
　　From going down the river !
Oh, powerless, but to weep and pray,
And grieve for one who, far away,
　　Had said his last farewell.

Weeping by the river,
 There came a blesséd time,
A solemn calm spread all around,
Making it seem like holy ground,
 Beside the silent river.
The world receding from our eyes,
Caught gleams of that dear land which lies
 In Canaan's happy clime !

And there, beside the river,
 Came lessons strange and sweet,
The perfect work of patience done,
The warfare finished, victory won
 With weak hands by the river !
The childlike fear, the clinging love,
The darkness brightened from above,
 The peace at Jesus' feet !

Waiting by the river,
 Through mingled night and day,
Sweet memories round our hearts we bring,
Of Jesus' love and heaven we sing,
 To soothe her by the river ;
And wept for one whose heart would break.
Be pitiful, for Jesus' sake,
 Father in heaven, we pray.

Standing by the river,
 We closed the weary eyes ;
In Jesus' arms we laid her down,
A lovely jewel for his crown.

He bore her through the river,
And clothed her in a robe so white,
Too beautiful for mortal sight,
And took her to the skies !

———◆———

The Beautiful Gate.

WHEN mysterious whispers are floating about,
　　And voices that will not be still
Shall summon me hence from the slippery shore
　　To the waves that are silent and still ;
When I look with changed eyes at the home of the blest,
　　Far out of the reach of the sea,
Will any one stand at that beautiful gate
　　Waiting and watching for me ?

There are friendless and suffering strangers around,
　　There are tempted and poor I must meet ;
There are dear ones at home I may bless with my love
　　There are wretched ones pacing the street ;
There are many unthought of, whom, happy and blest,
　　In the land of the good I shall see :
Will any of these at the beautiful gate
　　Be waiting and watching for me?

There are old and forsaken, who linger awhile
　　In the homes which their dearest have left,
And an action of love and a few gentle words
　　Might cheer the sad spirit bereft ;

But the reaper is near to the long-standing corn,
  The weary shall soon be set free ;
Will any of these at the beautiful gate
  Be waiting and watching for me ?

There are little ones glancing about on my path
  In need of a friend or a guide ;
There are dim little eyes looking up into mine,
  Whose tears could be easily dried ;
But Jesus may beckon the children away
  In the midst of their grief or their glee :
Will any of them at the beautiful gate
  Be waiting and watching for me ?

I may be brought there by the manifold grace
  Of the Saviour who loved to forgive,
Though I bless not the hungry ones near to my side,
  Only pray for myself while I live ;
But I think I should mourn o'er my selfish neglect,
  If sorrow in heaven can be,
If no one should stand at that beautiful gate
  Waiting and watching for me !

One by One.

THEY are gathering homeward from every land,
        One by one ;
As their weary feet touch the shining strand,
        One by one,

Their brows are enclosed in a golden crown,
Their travel-stained garments are all laid down,
And, clothed with white raiment, they rest on the mead,
Where the Lamb loveth his chosen to lead,
         One by one.

Before they rest they pass through the strife,
         One by one ;
Through the waters of death they enter life,
         One by one.
To some are the floods of the river still,
As they ford their way to the heavenly hill ;
To others the waves run fiercely and wild,
Yet all reach the home of the undefiled,
         One by one.

We too shall come to the river's side,
         One by one ;
We are nearer its waters each even-tide,
         One by one :
We can hear the noise and dash of the stream,
Now and again, through our life's deep dream ;
Sometimes the floods o'er the bank o'erflow,
Sometimes in ripples the small waves go,
         One by one.

Jesus ! Redeemer ! we look to thee,
         One by one ;
We lift up our voices tremblingly,
         One by one.

The waves of the river are dark and cold,
We know not the spots where our feet may hold;
Thou who didst pass through in deep midnight,
Strengthen us, send us the staff and the light,
   One by one.

Plant thou thy feet beside as we tread,
   One by one;
On thee let us lean each drooping head,
   One by one:
Let but thy mighty arm around us be twined,
We 'll cast all our fears and cares to the wind.
Saviour! Redeemer! with thee full in view,
Smilingly, gladsomely, shall we pass through,
   One by one.

Poor Man's Sunday.

WE thank thee, Lord, for one day,
  To look heaven in the face!
The poor have only Sunday;
  The sweeter is the grace.
'T is then they make the music
  That sings their week away,
Oh there 's a sweetness infinite
  In the poor man's Sabbath-day!

'T is as a burst of sunshine
  A tender fall of rain,
That set the barest life abloom,
  Make old hearts young again.

The dry and dusty roadside
With smiling flowers is gay;
'Tis open heaven one day in seven,
The poor man's Sabbath-day!

GERALD MASSEY

Going to Sunday-School.

ON Sunday morning early,
  While yet the grass is pearly;
    The air is bright and cool;
All clad in our best graces,
With rosy morning faces,
    We go to the Sunday-school!

To-day is life in blossom—
Heartsease in every bosom,
    And all is beautiful,
A spirit within us springing
At heaven's gate will be singing
    Thanks for the Sunday-school!

We sun us in its brightness;
We clothe us in its whiteness,
    As doth the wayside pool,
That holds from morn till even
Its little bit of heaven—
    The gladsome Sabbath-school!

Here learn we how to lighten
The heaviest lot, and brighten

The day most dark with dule,
And lay up childhood's treasure,
To reap immortal pleasure
    Even in a Sunday-school!

The summer earth rejoices,
With hers we lift our voices
    And heaven blends the whole,
And when God's angels cover us,
Drawing the darkness over us,
    They bless the Sunday-school!

GERALD MASSEY.

No Time to Pray.

NO time to pray!
  Oh, who so fraught with earthly care .
As not to give to humble prayer
    Some part of day?

    No time to pray!
What heart so clean, so pure within,
That needeth not some check from sin --
    Needs not to pray?

    No time to pray!
'Mid each day's danger, what retreat
More needful than the mercy-seat?
    Who need not pray?

No time to pray!
Must care or business' urgent call
So press us as to take it all,
            Each passing day?

No time to pray!
Then sure your record falleth short;
Excuse will fail you as resort
            On that last day.

What thought more drear
Than that our God his face should hide
And say, through all life's swelling tide,
            No time to hear!

Cease not to pray;
On Jesus as your all rely.
Would you live happy—happy die?
            Take time to pray.

The Sabbath Bell.

HOW sweetly through the lengthened dell,
    When wintry airs are mild and clear,
Floats chiming up the Sabbath bell,
    In softened echoes to the ear!
"Come, gentle neighbors, come away,"
So does the welcome summons say;
"Come, friends and kindred, 't is the time."
So seems to peal the Sabbath chime.

Done are the week's debasing cares,
   And worldly ways and worldly will,
And earth itself an aspect wears
   Like heaven, so bright, so pure, so still!
Hark, how by turns each mellow note,
Now low, now louder, seems to float,
And falling with the wind's decay,
Like softest music dies away!

"And now," it says, "where heaven resorts,
   Come with a meek and quiet mind;
Oh, worship in these earthly courts,
   But leave your earth-born thoughts behind."
Come, neighbors, while the Sabbath bell
Peals slowly up the winding dell,
Come, friends and kindred, let us share
The sweet and holy rapture there.

The Celestial Sabbath.

THE golden palace of my God,
   Towering above the clouds, I see,
Beyond the cherub's bright abode,
   Higher than angels' thoughts can be.
How can I in these courts appear,
   Without a wedding garment on?
Conduct me, thou Life-giver, there,
   Conduct me to thy glorious throne,
And clothe me with thy robes of light,
And lead me through sin's darksome night,
   My Saviour and my God.

Manna in the Night.

SILENTLY it fell,
 Whence, no man might tell,
  Like good dreams from heaven
  Unto mortals given,
  Like a snowy flock
Of strange sea-birds alighting on a shore of rock;
  Silent thus and bright,
  Fell the manna in the night.

  Silent thus and bright,
  In our starless night,
  God's sweet mercy comes
  All about our homes;
  Whence no man can see,
In a soft shower drifting, drifting ceaselessly,
  Till the morning light,
  Falls the manna in the night.

  Thus His mercy's crown,
  "Bread of life" came down.
  At our doors it fell,
  Whence no man might tell,
  Silent to the ground,
Softly shining thus through the darkness all around,
  Snowy, pure and white,
  Fell the manna in the night.

The Better Country.

SWEET place, sweet place alone,
  The court of God Most High,
The heaven of heavens, the throne
  Of spotless majesty !
The stranger homeward bends,
  And sigheth for his rest :
Heaven is my home ; my friends
  Lodge there in Abram's breast.
    O happy place !
      When shall I be,
      My God, with thee,
    To see thy face ?

Earth 's but a sorry tent
  Pitched for a few frail days,
A short-leased tenement ;
  Heaven 's still my song, my praise.
No tears from any eyes
  Drop in that holy choir ;
But death itself there dies,
  And sighs themselves expire.
    O happy place !
      When shall I be,
      My God, with thee,
    To see thy face ?

There should temptations cease;
  My frailties there should end:
There should I rest in peace,
  In the arms of my best Friend.
Jerusalem on high
  My song and city is,
My home whene'er I die,
  The centre of my bliss.
    O happy place!
      When shall I be,
      My God, with thee,
    To see thy face?

Thy walls, sweet city, thine,
  With pearls are garnishéd;
Thy gates with praises shine,
  Thy streets with gold are spread;
No sun by day shines there,
  Nor moon by silent night:
Oh no! these needless are;
  The Lamb 's the city's light.
    O happy place!
      When shall I be
      My God, with thee,
    To see thy face?

There dwells my Lord, my King,
  Judged here unfit to live;
There angels to him sing,
  And lowly homage give;

The Lamb's apostles there
  I might with joy behold;
The harpers I might hear
  Harping on harps of gold.
    O happy place!
      When shall I be,
      My God, with thee,
    To see thy face?

The bleeding martyrs, they
  Within those courts are found,
All clothed in pure array,
  Their scars with glory crowned.
Ah me! ah me! that I
  In Kedar's tents here stay!
No place like this on high!
  Thither, Lord, guide my way!
    O happy place!
      When shall I be,
      My God, with thee,
    To see thy face?   SAMUEL CROSSMAN

Jerusalem.

JERUSALEM the golden!
  I weary for one gleam
Of all thy glory folden
  In distance and in dream!

My thoughts, like palms in exile,
  Climb up to look and pray
For a glimpse of thy dear country
  That lies so far away.

Jerusalem the golden !
  When sunset's in the west,
It seems thy gate of glory,
  Thou city of the blest,
And midnight's starry torches,
  Through intermediate gloom,
Are waving with our welcome
  To thy eternal home !

Jerusalem the golden !
  There all our birds that flew,
Our flowers but half unfolden,
  Our pearls that turned to dew,
And all the glad life-music,
  Now heard no longer here,
Shall come again to greet us
  As we are drawing near.

Jerusalem the golden !
  I toil on, day by day ;
Heartsore each night with longing,
  I stretch my hands and pray,
That, 'mid thy leaves of healing,
  My soul may find her nest,
Where the wicked cease from troubling,
  The weary are at rest !   GERALD MASSEY

Pleasure in Heaven.

WILL it no pleasure be,
  When faith shall end in knowing,
Hope to fruition growing,
  The Saviour's face to see?
To learn from him the story,
What vict'ries won our glory—
  Will this no pleasure be?

Will it no pleasure be,
When friends who went before us
Our God shall there restore us,
  From pain and sickness free?
Where sorrows show no traces,
To meet their glad embraces,
  Will this no pleasure be?

Will it no pleasure be,
Where th' angel-chorus raises
To God most high their praises,
  With seraphs to agree?
And when the skies are ringing,
To join "Thrice holy!" singing,
  Will this no pleasure be?

Oh yes, there's pleasure there!
Away, earth's glittering bubbles,
Your joys are full of troubles,

Your bliss not worth the care
Then, friends, do not bewail me,
When heart and flesh shall fail me,
But think, there's pleasure there!

FROM THE GERMAN.

————◆————

Eternity!

ETERNITY, eternity,
How long art thou, eternity!
Yet hasteth on toward thee our life,
E'en as the war-steed to the strife,
The messenger toward home doth go,
Or ship to shore, or bolt from bow.

Eternity, eternity,
How long art thou, eternity!
As in a globe, so smooth and round,
Beginning ne'er and end are found,
Eternity, not more can we
Beginning find, or end, in thee.

Eternity, eternity,
How long art thou, eternity!
Thou art a ring of awful mould;
"For ever" is thy centre called,
And "Never" thy circumference wide;
For unto thee no end can tide.

Eternity, eternity,
How long art thou, eternity!
And if a little bird bore forth
One single sand-corn from the earth,
And took in thousand years but one,
Ere thou wert past, the world were gone!

Eternity, eternity,
How long art thou, eternity!
In thee, if every thousandth year,
An eye should drop one little tear,
To hold the water thence would grow,
Nor heaven nor earth were wide enow.

Eternity, eternity,
How long art thou, eternity?
Hear, man! So long as God shall reign,
So long continue hell and pain;
So long last heaven and joy also.
Oh, lengthened joy! oh, lengthened woe!

GERMAN

Talitha, Cumi!

TALITHA, Cumi!"
"Damsel, arise!"
And slowly open
Those death-sealed eyes.

With a name of endearment,
　Tender and soft—
Her mother had waked her
　From sleep with it oft—

He calls her spirit
　Beyond the tombs,
"Talitha, Cumi!"
　She hears and comes.

The portals of Hades,
　The gates of brass,
Which through the ages
　None living pass,

Before those accents
　Quake as with thunder,
Quiver like aspens,
　And part asunder;

Open like flowers
　Touched by the sun;
Yet through the portals
　Passeth but one.

Fearless came through them
　The soul of the child,
Saw him who called her,
　Knew him, and smiled.

"Talitha, Cumi!"
　　The Saviour spoke;
And as from light slumbers
　　The dead awoke.

MRS. CHARLES.

The Loved One Ever Nigh.

THOU art not lost to me, though coldly lying
　　　　Beneath the snows;
While thy pure spirit to the land is flying
　　　　Of blest repose.

Death has but loosed the bonds which oft forbade
　　　　thee
　　　　　　With me to be;
The grave holds only what could e'er have made
　　　　thee
　　　　　　A grief to me.

From all strange throngs thy loved familiar glances
　　　　Upon me smile,
And the lone hours when studious thought advances
　　　　Sweetly beguile.

Thou hearest when I speak with kind approval;
　　　　And from thy breast
My weary, aching head finds no removal—
　　　　But peaceful rest.

Mine eyes are holden—but my heart beholds thee
Thou join'st my prayer ;
And thy pure love in heavenly arms enfolds me
With guardian care.

Up thro' the way to God thou 'rt gently drawing
My faltering feet :
The veil grows thin ; near comes thy low voice calling ;
Soon we shall meet.

My Guest.

SPEECHLESS Sorrow sat with me ;
I was sighing wearily !
Lamp and fire were out ; the rain
Wildly beat the window pane ;
In the dark we heard a knock
And a hand was on the lock ;
One in waiting spake to me,
Saying sweetly,
"I am come to sup with thee !"

All my room was dark and damp ;
"Sorrow," said I, "trim the lamp ;
Light the fire, and cheer thy face ;
Set the guest-chair in its place."
And again I heard the knock ;
In the dark I found the lock :
"Enter, I have found the key !
Enter, Stranger,
Who art come to sup with me !"

Opening wide the door he came,
But I could not speak his name ;
In the guest-chair took his place,
But I could not see his face ;
When my cheerful fire was beaming,
When my little lamp was gleaming
And the feast was spread for three,
     Lo ! my Master
Was the guest that supped with me !

H. M. KIMBALL.

The Old Fisherman by the Sea.

AY, I was strong
  And able-bodied—loved my work ; but now
I am a useless hull : 't is time I sunk.
I am in all men's way ; I trouble them ;
I am a trouble to myself. But yet
I feel for mariners of stormy nights,
And feel for wives that watch ashore. Ay, ay,
If I had learning I would pray the Lord
To bring them in : but I 'm no scholar, no ;
Book-learning is a world too hard for me ;
But I make bold to say, 'O Lord ! good Lord !
I am a broken-down poor man, a fool
To speak to thee ; but in the book 't is writ,
As I hear say from others that can read,
How, when thou camest, thou didst love the sea,
And live with fisherfolk ; whereby 't is sure
Thou knowest all the peril they go through,
And all their trouble.

       " 'As for me, good Lord,
I have no boat ; I am too old—too old !
My lads are drowned : I buried my poor wife ;
My little lasses died so long ago
That mostly I forget what they were like.
Thou knowest, Lord, they were such little ones
I know they went to thee, but I forget
Their faces—though I missed them sore.

                  " 'O Lord,
I was a strong man ; I have drawn good food
And made good money out of thy great sea,
But yet I cried for them at nights ; and now
Although I be so old, I miss my lads.
And there be many folk this stormy night
Heavy with fear for theirs.   Merciful Lord,
Comfort them : save their honest boys, their pride,
And let them hear next ebb, the blessedest
Best sound—the boat keel grating on the sand.

   " 'I cannot pray with finer words.   I know
Nothing ; I have no learning, cannot learn—
Too old—too old !   They say. I want for naught,
I have the parish pay.

                " 'But I am dull
Of hearing, and the fire scarce warms me through.
God save me ! I have been a sinful man.
And save the lives of those that still can work,
For they are good to me ; ay, good to me.
But, Lord, I am a trouble ! and I sit,
And I am lonesome, and the nights are few

That any think to come and draw a chair,
And sit in my poor place and talk awhile.
Why should they come forsooth?   Only the wind
Knocks at my door.   Oh long and loud it knocks,
The only thing God made that has a mind
To enter in.'"

       Yea, thus the old man spake:
These were the last words of his aged mouth.
BUT ONE DID KNOCK!   One came to sup with him,
That humble, weak old man; knocked at his door
In the rough pauses of the laboring wind.
I tell you that ONE knocked while it was dark;

      What He said
In that poor place where he did talk awhile,
I cannot tell: but this I am assured,
That when the neighbors came the morrow morn,
What time the wind had bated, and the sun
Shone on the old man's floor, they saw the smile
He passed away in, and they said, "He looks
As he had woke and seen the face of Christ,
And with that rapturous smile held out his arms
To come to Him."　　　　　JEAN INGELOW.

———◆———

MY years crowd sail, and pass away
   Before me to eternity.
  How poorly freighted, Lord, are they
    With acts of faith and love to thee!

After the Rain.

THE old man sits 'neath the tall elm-trees,
  And watches the heavens with dreamy eyes,
While his white locks stir to the same cool breeze
  That scatters the silver along the skies.

The old man's eyelids are wet with tears—
  Tears of sweet pleasure and sweeter pain,
For his thoughts are driving back over the years
  Like beautiful clouds after life's long rain.

Sorrows that drowned all the springs of his life,
  Trials that crushed him with pitiless beat,
Storms of temptation and tempests of strife,
  Float o'er his memory—tranquil and sweet.

And the old man's spirit, made soft and bright
  By the long, long rain that bent him low,
Sees a vision of angels on wings of white,
  In the drooping clouds as they come and go.

Auld Man and Wife.

O HAPPY was the gloamin', when
  I gently wooed and won thee,
As through the shadows o' the glen
  The young moon smiled upon thee.
Thine e'en were like the stars aboon,
  Thy step was like the fairy,
And sweeter than the throstle's tune
  Was thy saft voice, my Mary.

Thy han' in mine, my cheek to thine,
  Our beating hearts thegither,
And mair than a' the warld beside
  Were we to ane anither.

Fu' mony a day we twa hae seen,
  Fu' mony a night o' sorrow;
And clouds that lowered the yester-e'en,
  Grew blacker on the morrow;
Yet never was the day sae sad,
  Nor night sae mirk and eerie,
But ae fond kiss could mak' us glad,
  My ain dear faithfu' Mary.
Thy han' in mine, my cheek to thine,
  Our beating hearts thegither,
The warld might frown, but what cared we,
  Sae we had ane anither?

And now as in the gloamin' sweet,
  When first my passion won thee,
I homeward come at e'en to meet
  And fondly gaze upon thee;
Tho' locks be gray on ilka brow,
  And feet be slow and wearie,
O ne'er to me sae dear wert thou,
  Nor I to thee, my Mary.
Thy han' in mine, my cheek to thine,
  Our beating hearts thegither,
Whate'er may change, thae hearts are still
  The same to ane anither.

The gloamin' dim o' passing life
  Is fa'ing gently o'er us ;
And here we sit, auld man and wife,
  Nor dread the night before us ;
For we maun lift to heaven hie
  A lightsome hope and cheerie,
Nor fear to lay us doon and die,
  And wak' aboon, my Mary.
Thy han' in mine, my cheek to thine,
  Our faithfu' hearts thegither,
Welcome be death to tak' the ane,
  Gin he will tak' the ither !   DR. BETHUNE.

Nearer to Life's Winter, Wife.

NEARER to life's winter, wife,
  We are drawing nearer,
Memories of our blessed spring
  Growing dearer, dearer.

Through the summer's heats we 've toiled,
  Through the autumn weather,
We have often passed, sweet wife,
  Hand in hand together.

Time was, hearts were, well as feet,
  Lighter, I remember ;
April's locks of gold are turned
  Silver, this November.

Flowers are fewer than at first,
  And the way grows drearer,
For unto life's winter, wife,
  We are drawing nearer.

Nearer to life's end, sweet wife,
  We are drawing nearer ;
The last mile-stone on our way
  To our sight grows clearer.

Some whose hands we held grew faint,
  And lay down to slumber ;
Looking backwards, we to-day
  All their graves may number.

Heights we 've sought we 've failed to climb
  Fruits we 've failed to gather ;
But what matter, since we 've still
  Jesus and each other ?

Crossing the Moor,

I AM thinking of the glen, Johnny,
  And the little gushing brook —
Of the birds upon the hazel copse,
  And violets in the nook.
I am thinking how we met, Johnny,
  Upon the little bridge :
You had a garland on your arm
  Of flag-flowers and of sedge.

You placed it in my hand, Johnny,
    And held my hand in yours;
You only thought of that, Johnny,
    But talked about the flowers.
We lingered long alone, Johnny,
    Above that shaded stream;
We stood as though we were entranced
    In some delicious dream.

It was not all a dream, Johnny,
    The love we thought of then,
For it hath been our life and light
    For threescore years and ten.
But ah! we dared not speak it,
    Though it lit our cheeks and eyes;
So we talked about the news, Johnny
    The weather, and the skies.

At last I said, "Good night, Johnny!
    And turned to cross the bridge,
Still holding in my trembling hand
    The pretty wreath of sedge.
But you came on behind, Johnny,
    And drew my arm in yours,
And said, "You must not go alone
    Across the barren moors."

Oh, had they been all flowers, Johnny,
    And full of singing birds,
They could not have seemed fairer
    Than when listening to those words

The new moon shone above, Johnny,
　The sun was nearly set ;
The grass that crisped beneath our **feet**
　The dew had slightly wet :

One robin, late abroad, Johnny,
　Was winging to its nest ;
I seem to see it now, Johnny,
　The sunshine on its breast.
You put your arm around me,
　You clasped my hand in yours,
You said, " So let me guard you
　Across these lonely moors."

At length we reached the field, Johnny,
　In sight of father's door ;
We felt that we must part there ;
　Our eyes were brimming o'er ;
You saw the tears in mine, Johnny,
　I saw the tears in yours :
" You 're been a faithful guard, Johnny,
　I said, "across the moors."

Then you broke forth in a gush, Johnny
　Of pure and honest love,
While the moon looked down upon you
　From her holy throne above,
And you said, " We need a guide, Ellen
　To lead us o'er life's moors ;
I 've chosen you for mine, Ellen,
　Oh, would that I were yours !"

We parted with a kiss, Johnny,
    The first, but not the last;
I feel the rapture of it yet,
    Though threescore years have passed;
And you kissed my golden curls, Johnny,
    That now are silver gray,
And whispered, "We are one, Ellen,
    Until our dying day!"

That dying day is near, Johnny,
    But we are not dismayed;
We have but one dark moor to cross,
    Why need we be afraid?
We've had a hard life's row, Johnny,
    But our heavenly rest is sure;
And sweet the love that waits us there,
    When we have crossed the moor!

MRS. S. F. MAYO.

Snow.

THE summer comes, and the summer goes,
    Wild-flowers are fringing the dusty lanes,
    The sparrows go darting through fragrant rains,
And all of a sudden—it snows!

Dear heart! our lives so happily flow,
    So lightly we heed the flying hours,
    We only know winter is gone by the flowers,
We only know winter is come by the snow!

T. B. ALDRICH.

First and Last.

JUST come from heaven, how bright and fair
  The soft locks of the baby's hair !
As if the unshut gates still shed
The shining halo round his head.

Just entering heaven, what sacred snows
Upon the old man's brow repose !
For there the opening gates have thrown
The glory from the great white throne.

H. P. SPOFFORD.

"I Never Cast a Flower Away."

I NEVER cast a flower away,
  The gift of one who cared for me—
A little flower—a faded flower,
  But it was done reluctantly.

I never looked a last adieu
  To things familiar, but my heart
Shrank with a feeling almost pain,
  Even from their lifelessness to part.

I never spoke the word "Farewell,"
  But with an utterance faint and broken ·
An earth-sick longing for the time
  When it shall never more be spoken.

MRS. SOUTHEY.

Not Knowing.

I KNOW not what shall befall me.
　　God hangs a mist o'er my eyes,
And each step in my onward path
　　He makes new scenes to rise,
And every joy he sends me
　　Comes as a sweet surprise.

I see not a step before me,
　　As I tread on another year,
But the past is still in God's keeping
　　The future his mercy shall clear,
And what looks dark in the distance,
　　May brighten as I draw near.

For perhaps the dreaded future
　　Has less bitter than I think :
The Lord may sweeten the waters
　　Before I stoop to drink ;
Or if Marah must be Marah,
　　He will stand beside its brink.

It may be he has, waiting
　　For the coming of my feet,
Some gift of such rare value,
　　Some joy so strangely sweet,
That my lips shall only tremble
　　With the thanks they cannot speak

Oh, restful, blissful ignorance!
  'T is blesséd not to know:
It keeps me still in those arms
  Which will not let me go,
And hushes my soul to rest
  In the bosom that loved me so!

So I go on—not knowing:
  I would not if I might,
Rather walking with God in the dark
  Than going alone in the light:
Rather walking with him by faith
  Than walking alone by sight.

My heart shrinks back from trials
  Which the future may disclose,
Yet I never had a sorrow
  But what the dear Lord chose;
So I send the coming tears back,
  With the whispered word—"He knows!"

M. J. BRAI FLD.

"I Sleep, but my Heart Waketh!"

IT is the night; the lights are burning low,
    . The house is still,
  And through the silent chambers come and go,
      At their own wayward will,
  The dreams that thrill the night, with murmurings
  Of voices, mingled with a rush of wings.

And going through the house we are aware
    Of dreams upon the wall,
Of visions passing up the shadowy stair,
    And through the vacant hall ;
And every sleeper in his darkened room,
Is busy with his guests, in joy or gloom.

Then come dear living ones across the sea,
    From distant lands ;
Then come the holy dead, in ecstasy,
    With lilies in their hands,
And looks more sweet, to these poor hearts of ours,
Than even the fragrance of eternal flowers !

And dearer than the living ones, that dwell
    Beyond the throbbing sea,
And dearer than the dead, whose voices swell
    The heavenly melody,
One visiteth his people in the night,
Who giveth songs, and makes the darkness bright.

"I sleep ; yet evermore my heart doth wake,
    Within the veil ;
The voice of my belovéd ! hear it break
    Across the moonlight pale :
He is come down to comfort me awhile,
And cheer the sad night with his tender smile."

And when the days and nights of earth are flown
    And I lie dead,
Then come and write, dear friends, upon the stone
    Above my quiet head,

" I sleep ; yet far upon the crystal sea,
My heart is waking—waking, Lord, with thee !"

For I shall sleep beneath the steadfast sky,
 So free from care,
That evermore my hands may folded lie,
 As if in prayer :
And evermore the sealéd eyelids keep
The secret of dim eyes, that joyful sleep.

And, whilst I sleep, behold ! my heart will wake,
 And sing its perfect song,
In thy sweet presence, Master, for whose sake
 It watched and waited long ;
And evermore thy deathless love shall be
The treasure of the heart that loveth thee ! B. M.

Jesus Knows!

I CANNOT understand, when o'er time's ocean
 My life barque sailed,
Why tempests came, and why in dim confusion
 My way seemed veiled.
The reasons are not clear to my weak vision ;
 I look in vain
For that fair past, and for those fields Elysian
 I thought to gain.
But this is plain, God saw it best, and therefore
 The storm arose :
And though I cannot see the why nor wherefore,
 Yet Jesus knows.

I cannot tell why, when the day seemed clearest,
    Dark clouds should lower :
Nor why the hopes that my fond heart held dearest
    Failed in that hour :
I know not why the morning's glorious shining
    Was veiled ere noon,
Nor why the fragrant garlands love was twining
    Should fade so soon.
But this I know ; though God his why and wherefore
    Does not disclose,
His purposes are ever best, and therefore
    My Jesus knows.

Much, much there is, to our poor human vision
    Shrouded in gloom ;
Much that, when questioned by our weak decision,
    Seems saddest doom.
Many the treasures that we mourn departed
    From our fond hold,
Leaving us desolate and broken-hearted,
    With griefs untold.
We cannot fathom yet the why nor wherefore
    Of joys or woes,
But our dear Lord does ever right, and therefore
    My Jesus knows.

An Ended Earthly Life.

YES! the day has been full of labor,
　　But now is the daylight past;
And the journey was very toilsome
　　But the journey is over at last.

Lo! the pilgrim's staff is broken
　　And the sandals are laid aside;
"I am come to the gate," said our father;
　　"Will they hear on the other side?

"I have only a little token,
　　'T was given me long ago:
But it came from the dear Redeemer,
　　Who liveth and loveth—I know!"

Softly he whispered the watchword,
　　As he knocked at the gate of the King
And I think that the shining angels
　　Must have hasted to let him in.

For just as the terrible shadow
　　Was veiling the dear old face,
There fell o'er its marble features
　　A glory of perfect peace.

It smoothed away from the forehead
　　The folds and the lines of care;
And touched with its brightening halo
　　The tresses of silvered hair.

For a moment the voice of our weeping
Was hushed at the glorious sight,
For the fearful shadow had passed away
And "the evening time was light!"

Old Age Longing for Home.

A SONG of a boat:
  There was once a boat on a billow;
Lightly she rocked to her port remote,
And the foam was white in her wake, like snow,
And her frail mast bowed when the breeze would blow,
  And bent like a wand of willow.

I shaded my eyes one day when this boat
  Went courtesying over the billow,
I marked her course till a dancing mote
She faded out on the moonlit foam,
And I stayed behind in the dear loved home;
And my thoughts all day were about the boat
  And in dreams upon my pillow.

I pray you hear my song of a boat,
  For it is but short.
My boat, you shall find none fairer afloat
  In river or port.
Long I looked out for the lad she bore,
  On the open desolate sea,
But I think he sailed to the heavenly shore,
  For he came not back to me—
                    Ah me!

A song of a nest.
There was once a nest in a hollow;
Down in the mosses and knot-grass pressed,
Soft and warm, and full to the brim—
Vetches leaned over it purple and dim,
　With buttercup buds to follow.

I pray you hear my song of a nest,
　For it is not long:
You shall never light, in a summer quest
　The bushes among—
Shall never light on a prouder sitter,
　A fairer nestful, nor ever know
A softer sound than their tender twitter,
　That wind-like did come and go.

I had a nestful once of my own,
　Oh happy, happy I!
Right dearly I loved them; but when they were
　　grown
　They spread out their wings to fly,
Oh one after one they flew away
　Far up to the heavenly blue,
To the better country, the upper day,
　And—I wish I was going too.

I pray you what is the nest to me,
　My empty nest?
And what is the shore where I stood to see
　My boat sail down to the west?

Can I call that home where I anchor yet
    Though my good man has sailed?
Can I call that home where my nest was set,
    Now all its hope hath failed?
Nay but the port where my sailor went,
    And the land where my nestlings be;
There is the home where my thoughts are sent,
    The only home for me—
                    Ah me!

                                        JEAN INGELOW

The Nest.

I BUILT my nest by a pleasant stream
    That glided on with a smile in its gleam,
        Bringing me gold that was sumless;
Ah me! but the floods came drowning one day.
And swept my nest with its wealth away;
        I in the world was homeless!

I built my nest in a gay green tree,
And the summer of life went merrily
        With us! we were birds of a feather!
But the leaves soon fell, and my pretty ones flew,
And through my nest the bitter winds blew;
        'T was bare in the wildest weather.

I built my nest under heaven's high eaves;
No rising of floods, no falling of leaves,

Can mock my heart's endeavor;
Waters may wash, and breezes may blow,
In the bosom of Rest I shall smile, I shall know
My nest is safe for ever.   G. MASSEY.

My Ain Countree!

I AM far frae my hame, an' I'm weary oftenwhiles,
For the langed for hame-bringing an' my Father's
   welcome smiles;
I 'll ne'er be fu' content, until my een do see
The gowden gates of heaven, an' my ain countree !

The earth is flecked with flowers, many-tinted, fresh
   and gay,
The birdies warble blithely, for my Father made them
   sae ;
But these lights an' these soun's will be naething to me,
When I hear the angels singing in my ain countree !

I 've his gude word of promise, that some gladsome day
   the King
To his ain royal palace his banished hame will bring ;
Wi' een an' wi' hearts running over we shall see
The King in his beauty in our ain countree !

My sins have been mony, an' my sorrows ha' been sair,
But there they 'll nae mair vex me, nor be remembered
   mair,
His bluid has made me white, his hand shall dry mine ee,
When he brings me back at length to my ain countree '

14

Like a bairn to its mither, a wee birdie to its nest,
I wad fain be ganging noo unto my Saviour's breast ;
For he gathers in his bosom, witless, worthless lambs
        like me,
An' he carries them himsel' to his ain countree !

He is faithfu' that hath promised, he 'll surely come
        again ;
He 'll keep his tryst wi' me, at what hour I dinna ken ;
But he bids me still to watch, an' ready aye to be
To gang at ony moment to my ain countree !

So I 'm watching, aye, an' singing o' my hame as I wait,
For the sounin' o' his foot-fa' this side the gowden gate.
God gie his grace to ilk ane who listens noo to me,
That we a' may gang in gladness to our ain countree !

MISS M. A. LEE.

The Lowly Life.

A LITTLE flower so lowly grew,
    So lonely was it left,
That heaven looked like an eye of blue,
    Down in its rocky cleft.

What could the little flower do,
    In such a darksome place,
But try to reach that eye of blue
    And climb to kiss heaven's face?

And there's no life so lone and low
But strength may still be given,
From narrowest lot on earth to grow
The straighter up to heaven.

GERALD MASSEY

Christ is all.

I ENTERED once a home of care,
For age and penury were there,
  Yet peace and joy withal ;
I asked the lonely mother whence
Her helpless widowhood's defence :
  She told me Christ was all.

I stood beside a dying bed,
Where a sweet infant drooped his head,
  Waiting for Jesus' call ;
I marked his smile, 't was sweet as May,
And as his spirit passed away,
  He whispered, "Christ is all."

I saw the martyr at the stake,
And no fierce flames his faith could shake,
  Nor death his soul appal ;
I asked him whence such strength was given,
He looked triumphantly to heaven,
  And answered "Christ is all."

I saw the gospel herald go
To Afric's sand and Greenland's snow,
  To save from Satan's thrall ;

Nor hope nor life he counted dear;
'Midst want and perils owned no fear;
   He felt that Christ was all.

I dreamed that hoary time had fled,
And earth and sea gave up their dead,
   And fire dissolved this ball;
I saw the church's ransomed throng,
I heard the burden of their song:
   'T was, "Christ is all in all!"

Then come to Jesus, come to-day.
"Come!" Father, Son, and Spirit say;
   The Bride repeats the call.
Come, he has blood for all your stains;
Come, he has balm for all your pains;
   Come, Christ is all in all!

No Dream!

FAIR in the east the rosy morning breaks,
And Jacob trembling and amazed awakes.

"O wondrous dream! O vision passing fair!
O holy sacred spot! the Lord was there!"

He grasps his pilgrim staff and onward hies,
Hope in his smile and courage in his eyes.

And yet, if asked what made his heart so light,
"'T was but a dream, a vision of the night."

  *   *   *   *   *   *   *

Here, with my pilgrim scrip, and staff in hand,
I walk like Jacob through a stranger land.

Rough is the path, the journey long and drear,
And yet I go with courage and good cheer.

What makes my steps so free, my heart so light?
Ah! was it all a vision of the night?

My faith must fix on things unseen, unknown,
My hopes must rest on Jesus' word alone.

And there are dreary hours when it may seem
All I have loved and hoped was but a dream.

Yet even then a whisper soft and low
Speaks to my inmost heart, "It is not so!

"That was no baseless dream which Faith believed:
The vision was not false which Hope received."

My father's God shall guide me with his hand,
Till the poor pilgrim gains his fatherland.

And when at last on Jacob's couch I lie—
A stone my pillow, and my tent the sky—

Then shall the gates of light again unclose,
And happy angels call me from repose;

Then all the past a bright reverse shall seem,
Heaven the reality, and earth the dream.

                                        KARL GEROK.

In Paradise.

OH, Paradise must fairer be
  Than any spot below!
My spirit pines for liberty;
  Now let me thither go!
In Paradise for ever clear
  The stream of love is flowing;
For every tear that I shed here
  A pearl therein is glowing.

In Paradise alone is rest,
  Joy-breathing, woe-dispelling;
A heavenly wind fans every breast
  Within that happy dwelling.
For every wounding thorn below
  A rose shall blossom there,
And sweeter flowers than earth can show
  Shall twine around my hair.

And every joy that, budding, died,
  Shall open there in bloom,
And Spring in all her flowery pride
  Shall waken from the tomb,
And all the joys shall meet me there
  For which my heart was pining,
Like golden fruit in gardens fair,
  And flowers for ever shining.

My youth that fled so soon away,
 And left me sad, decaying,
Shall there be with me every day,
 With bright wings round me playing ;
All hopes, all wishes, all the love
 I sighed for, pined for, ever,
Shall bloom around me there above,
 And last with me for ever !   RÜCKERT.

Fragments from Herrick.

HUMBLE we must be, if to heaven we go ;
 High is the roof there, but the gate is low.

GOD, when he takes my goods and chattels hence,
 Gives me a portion, giving patience.
What is in God is God ; if so it be
He patience gives, he gives himself to me.

GOD from our eyes all teares hereafter wipes,
 And gives his children kisses then, not stripes.

GOD gives to none so absolute an ease,
 As not to know or feel some grievances.

NO man is tempted so, but may o'ercome,
 If that he has a will to masterdom.

CHRIST took our nature on him, not that he
   'Bove all things loved it for its puritie ;
No ! but he drest him with our human trim,
Because our flesh stood most in need of him.

———•———

WHEN once the soule has lost her way,
   Oh, then, how restless does she stray !
And having not her God for light,
How does she erre in endless night !

———•———

HEAVEN is most faire, but fairer He
   That made that fairest canopie.

———•———

IN vain our labors are, whate'er they bo,
   Unless God gives
                        The Benedicite.

INDEX OF CONTENTS.

INDEX OF FIRST LINES.